EverWar UNIVERSE

KNIGHTS & LORDS

WORKS BY TY'RON W. C. ROBINSON II

BOOKS

DARK TITAN UNIVERSE SAGA

MAIN SERIES

Dark Titan Knights
The Resistance Protocol
Tales of the Scattered
Tales of the Numinous
Day of Octagon
Crossbreed
Heaven's Called

Forthcoming

The Resistance/Protectors War
Underworld
Magicks and Mysticism

SPIN-OFFS

In A Glass of Dawn: The Casebook of Travis Vail
Maveth: Bloodsport

Forthcoming

The Curse of The Mutant-Thing
Trail of Vengeance
War of The Thunder Gods

THE HAUNTED CITY SAGA

The Legendary Warslinger: The Haunted City I
Battle of Astolat: A Haunted City Prequel (KOBO Exclusive)
Redemption of the Lost: The Haunted City II
Consequences of the Suffering: The Haunted City III (Forthcoming)

SYMBOLUM VENATORES

Symbolum Venatores: The Gabriel Kane Collection
Hod: A Symbolum Venatores Book
Symbolum Venatores: War of The Two Kingdoms (Forthcoming)

OTHER BOOKS

Lost in Shadows: A Novel
Lost in Shadows: Remastered
Accounts of The Dead Days
The Book of The Elect
Hallow Sword: Cursed(KOBO Exclusive)
Dark Titan Omnibus: Volume 1
The Extended Age Omnibus
Frightened!: The Beginning
Dark Titan Omnibus: Volume 2 (Forthcoming)

KNIGHTS & LORDS

TYRON W. C. ROBINSON II

<u>BOC</u>
BATTLE OF CAELUM

<u>AOC</u>
AFTER BATTLE OF CAELUM

<u>THE ANCIENT COVENANT</u>
<u>IMPERIUM OF THE DEKAR</u>
<u>CAVALIER CIVIL WAR</u>
<u>WAR OF HELIO</u>
KNIGHT RAYEN AND THE CAVALIER OF LITHIOS
KNIGHT RAYEN AND THE SEARCH FOR LADY IYERA
YABEL, THE KNIGHT OF THE SALVATION
YABEL AND THE LOST GRAIL
AMRAN, THE PRINCE OF SINSTOR
<u>RISE OF THE SUPREMACY</u>
<u>ORDER OF THE VIPER</u>
LORDS OF THE VIPER
<u>THE ADVANCED COVENANT</u>
THE ANCIENT KNIGHTS OF ELYON
<u>ORDER OF THE DAMNED</u>
<u>ZORTH WARS</u>
<u>THE INSURGENCY</u>
<u>KNIGHTS OF THE SUPREMACY</u>
<u>ORDER WAR</u>
<u>A DARK MOON</u>
<u>THE JUDGMENT OCCURANCE</u>
<u>THE INTERSTELLUS WAR</u>
<u>HERITAGE</u>

CONTENTS

KNIGHT RAYEN
AND THE CAVALIER OF LITHIOS
A CHIVALRIC ROMANCE OF THE *EVER WAR*
UNIVERSE

720 BOC
720 YEARS DURING THE *BATTLE OF CAELUM*

"Before the world you've known, there existed an age of extraordinary proportions." - The High One

I
THE CHALLENGE OF THE STRANGER

The Knights of the Covenant celebrate their Feast of Pesakh within the tabernacle of the Tropolton Temple of the Avior and The High One. During the feast, the Knights and the Tropolton residents all celebrate, sing, and dance to The High One. They give him thanks for the Avior and his protection around those who believe. The Knights take center stage, dancing and celebrating the Feast.

While they danced within the walls of the temple. The front gates of proportion had opened and a man, dressed in white armor with a light bluish green cloak hanging from his neck to his back, riding on a pale horse with a bluish green noseband leather bridle and saddle. The man's face was covered by his helmet and his eyes weren't visible, but his aura presented an energy of coldness and anger. He made his way down the streets of Tropolton towards the temple where he could see the Knights and residents within the walls celebrating.

"This is a Feast to enjoy, Knights." said one Knight, holding his cup up. "To The High One!"

1

"To The High One!" The Knights shouted with joy.

They all clapped their cups together and drank. While drinking, the surroundings became quiet. The music had silenced, and the joyous voices were ceased. The Knights could feel there was something wrong. They each lowered their cups and in front of them, standing at the temple doors was the man on the pale horse. He stopped and stood in front of them, quiet and still. The Knights quickly command the residents to move away from the area as they surround the armored man.

"Who are you to trespass on this Feast?" A Knight said, holding out his aduroblade, which glows with a yellow aura.

"I am The Cavalier of Lithios." The armored man said. "I am here to offer the Knights of the Covenant a challenge."

"What is this challenge you present to us?"

"Face me in combat. Within your temple walls. If you defeat me, take my weapon and decapitate me. If you lose, I will decapitate you."

The Knights looked at each other. Each trying to wonder which one will take the challenge of The Cavalier of Lithios. While they stood and spoke to each other concerning the challenge, a young Knight of the Covenant stood up from the temple walls and approached the eyesight of The Cavalier. The Knights turned and seen the young Knight facing The Cavalier. Their eyes locked onto each other. Both of passion and fear.

"I, Knight Rayen, accept your challenge."

"I see you have little armor attached to your tunic uniform."

"Someone as I will not require much protection. Shall we proceed with the challenge?"

"Surely."

Knight Rayen reached to the left side of his waist, grabbing the handle of his aduroblade and pulls it out from its sheath. The blade possesses a white color and glows with a gold aura. The Cavalier laughed as he reached to his back and raised up an axe. An aduroaxe. The axe was of a bluish color and the energy surrounding the axe's head was coated in a green energy. It gave off the sound of surging electricity.

"Are you ready, Knight."

"I am."

Rayen and The Cavalier clash into combat with their aduro weapons. Twirling and swiping their weapons through the air toward one another. The Knights stood back as did the residents, all watching the duel take place within the center of the temple. Rayen threw slashes and swipes toward The Cavalier, who took them with his aduroaxe. He kicked Rayen in his abdomen and went to decapitate him, but Rayen raised up his aduroblade, which intercepted the aduroaxe. The Cavalier chuckled underneath his helmet. Rayen could hear his deep and graveling voice underneath it.

"Why don't you show us your face?" Rayen asked.

"Why should I."

Their aduro weapons clashing with one another as they give off the scent of a burning sensation. Both appear to slowly take several gasps of air before The Cavalier shoved Rayen from his aduroaxe and went for another swipe, which Rayen intercepted with his aduroblade again. Rayen kicked The Cavalier in his leg, which he fell down to one knee. Rayen raised his aduroblade and swiped the aduroaxe from The Cavalier's hand. The axe fell to the gold floors of the temple and its greenish aura evaporated.

"You've been defeated." Rayen said, placing his aduroblade back into its sheath.

"I have been." The Cavalier said, taking several breaths. "Now, finish me off. Complete the challenge, young Knight."

Rayen reached down to the floor and grabbed The Cavalier's aduroaxe. He held it in his hands as its aura began to glow around the head. The Cavalier looked up at Rayen, who could now see his eyes and they were cold. Cold as a snowy field. His eyes gave off the same feeling of his aura.

"Do it." The Cavalier said, hanging his head low.

Rayen raised up the aduroaxe and slammed it down, decapitating The Cavalier as his head fell to the floor and rolled over toward the wall. The room was quiet. Then, suddenly, a loud roar came from the residents who ran over to Rayen and praised him for his victory. The Knights approach Rayen with glad tidings and smiles.

"You completed the challenge of the stranger." said a Knight.

"I did what was necessary."

As they celebrated and praised Rayen's victory. The Cavalier's body arose from the ground. Rayen looked over and stared, seeing the headless body standing on its feet, facing him. The Knights and residents noticed Rayen's face and turned, also seeing the headless body facing them. The residents ran out of the temple in horror, leaving only the Knights to remain. The Cavalier's body walked over to the wall where his head had rolled over by. He picked up his head and placed it back onto his shoulders. The head regenerated with the neck and the wound was no more. He turned to Rayen and only stared at him.

"Young Knight. You have indeed completed the challenge that I presented to you. Now, you must accept your part in the challenge."

"Which is of what?"

"Three days before your New Year of Pesakh, you must present yourself on Lithios. In front of the Lithiosian Castle and enter its tabernacle. There you will face me in another duel and this time, you will be the one decapitated."

Rayen is silent. Not a word spoken. Nor an action witnessed. He turned and faced the Knights, who turned and watched The Cavalier go atop his pale horse. The Cavalier looked at Rayen once more.

"I expect to see you there, young Knight."

The pale horse neighed, and the Cavalier was gone from their sight and rode off back down the streets ot Tropolton and vanished as it exited the city's gates. Within the temple walls, Rayen held the aduroaxe of The Cavalier. The other Knights went to gaze at the weapon, not seeing one of such kind since the late Civil Wars. They were particularly impressed by its bluish color and its green aura, which appeared to be of a mineral not known of the living realm.

II
RAYEN'S TRIALS AND TRIBULATIONS

Throughout the remainder of the year, nearing its end and inching closer to Pesakh, the New Year, Rayen was praised and cheered throughout the year as the Knight who defeated The Cavalier of Lithios. The residents of Tropolton cheered him and loved him. They raised him up above some Knights who came before him. The other Knights of the Covenant watched on and congratulated Rayen on his victory, though, they could see the worrying within his being. The fear of being killed in a matter of months. The possibility of losing the next duel and losing his head.

For most of the year, Rayen stayed to himself at times within his chamber. He would pray to The High One for guidance and understanding concerning his future travel to Lithios, a planet he didn't know existed until the arrival of The Cavalier. During the year, he prepared himself mentally and physically. Learning new techniques of aduroblade combat.

Training with the Knights and the Palawan of the Abhdi. One day, he later sat down with an Elder Knight, which he was known as for his name was never given to those younger than his age. The Elder Knight had a presence with him. He dressed like the Ancient Knights of old and knew their names as if he lived among them. He witnessed the Cavalier Civil War and the wars before it. Some would believe he lived during the era when the Battle of Caelum first began.

Rayen would visit the Elder Knight within his closed room of the temple. He would sit in front of him and ask him for assistance and learning. Rayen would mostly ask of history details and how to increase the power of the Avior, to use it better in combat and with discernment of himself and others around him. The Elder Knight, who walked slowly with a limp in his right leg, patted Rayen on his shoulder and smiled at him. Showing relief for his being.

"I know you're worrying about your well-being, young one. But, I tell you, do not fear. For when you fear, the Dekar creeps in unaware and its settlers will come and seduce you. Giving you over to its dark power. Keep hope alive within you and the Avior will settle things in their correct way."

"But what shall I do when I step into the world of Lithios? How will I overcome The Cavalier this time?"

"By the Avior you will and your honorable feats of strength and valor. You, young one, are a different breed of Abhdi Knight than I have witnessed before. You face evil in the face without fear. You showed your people you can protect them and look how they've praised you for your heroic deed. When you head out on your quest to Lithios, do not hesitate. For the darker forces will present to you trials and tribulations that will interfere with your mission. Do not take heed to them, for they will come in a variety of forms. Forms that someone of your age must fight against. Surpass the distractions and defeat The Cavalier once and for all."

Rayen nodded and smiled at the Elder Knight and left his presence. He would continue to visit the Elder Knight each day, learning more and more about what he will find himself facing when he makes himself present on Lithios. Throughout the weeks, he continued to train alone and with the other Knights. One day, there was an invasion of Imperial Viper Knights, who came down and attacked the city. Rayen and the Knights went out and faced them. Defeating them in quick secession. The Elder Knight told them that the Viper Knights were a test from the Viper Lords, who were seeing how powerful the younger Knights were and had become.

The months were coming to a close and Rayen was preparing himself even more. Surpassing his own limits of training and learning. He studied the planet of Lithios, from what was told to him by the Elder Knight. His aduroblade skills were enhanced to where he could now use the blade with the Avior alone, something the Knights have not done since the Ancient Covenant had begun. Rayen continued his praying and even proceeded into fasting to prepare himself for the coming duel.

The Elder Knight watched Rayen exceed in his training, surpassing all of the Knights of the Covenant that were aligned with him. They cheered him on as his training continued and they guided him with his learning. He would walk outside of the temple and speak with the residents who needed help and he would aid them in their troubles. Using the Avior, he would heal them of sicknesses. Diseases were uncommon on Helio since the late days of the Ancient Covenant.

Rayen had looked at the calendar one day and noticed his day of visitation was coming the following week. He continued to train, pray, fast, and help others. The days had passed him by and he was on the brink of the New Year. Rayen went into his chamber one night. Down on both his knees and prayed to The High One.

"Abba, I ask of you once more, to guide me on this journey to Lithios. A world that I am unfamiliar with in its true nature. I do not know what I will be faced against when I get there, but I trust in you to stand by me with all my heart and spirit. Lead me through the planet that I may finish this challenge once and for all. Give me an increase of the Avior that I may exceedingly complete this challenge that I have accepted out of honor and dignity. I ask of you, to give me the strength. That all of this will be over."

After praying, Rayen laid down atop his bed and slept. For when the sunrise would come, he would be ready to travel to Lithios and face The Cavalier one last time.

III
THE CHALLENGE OF THE OUTSIDER

Rayen had awoke as the sunlight had glared over his face. Looking outside toward the grassy fields of Tropolton, he prepared himself for the journey ahead. He prayed that morning and dressed himself in a brown tunic with a brownish-red cloak. He grabbed his aduroblade and proceeded out of his chamber. Upon walking out, the Elder Knight was standing by his door, waiting for him. He smiled at him and he placed his arm around him, both walking towards the exit.

"Are you prepared for this, young one?"

"Yes, my Elder, I am. I will complete this mission and I will return here a man of victory and honor."

"Also, a hero to your people."

"Make us proud and give glory to The High One."

"I will do so."

Rayen said his goodbyes to the residents of Tropolton and to his fellow Knights as he went into one of Helio Sor ships and took off into the air, heading out into the depths of space to Lithios. Flying through the dark vacuum of space by himself for the first time, Rayen took sight at the worlds that were sitting around him. He recognized many of them from his studies. He looked at the digital map that sat in front of him near the ship control panel. He gazed at the map and a dot appeared onto the map, titled "Star 114".

10

"Ah, that is where Lithios is located. I'll have to go into hyperspace."

He placed the controls onto hyperspace and the ship moved with a quick pull, being sucked into the wormhole and vanished from the sector that he was recently in called Sector 333. The Helio Sor ship flew through the hyperspace, which appeared to look like trillions of stars stretched out amongst the surroundings. They gave off a bluish light with a mixture of white and silver.

He continued to go through hyperspace and looked at the map, seeing himself inching closer toward Lithios. He pulled back the handle and exited the hyperspace, finding himself in the sector of Star 114 and right in front of him was Lithios. A world colored in white. The planet looked like a cold and damp place from the outside.

"So, that's what it looks like, huh."

Rayen flew closer to the planet and as he proceeded to enter its atmosphere, the surroundings became cold and started to freeze in an instant. The planet's atmosphere was of a temperature to where even the flying creatures would freeze immediately. He slowly flew the ship through the atmosphere before breaking through the planet's ice clouds and behold, he gazed his eyes toward the ground. Covered in large amounts of snow. He could see trees, mountains, and what looked like small communities scattered across the grounds of Lithios.

Rayen looked around for a proper place to land the ship and decided to place it near the trees, to hide it from residents who may be residing on the icy planet. He exited the ship, his face shrouded by the hood of his cloak. His eyes covered with goggles. He placed his aduroblade to his side as he walked out of the ship. He gazed around at the surroundings and looked out into the horizon where he could see the top of the Lithiosian Castle.

"Here I go." He said as he took his first step through the snowy grounds.

Rayen walked and he walked through the heavy snow. Picking up his feet with his strength and fighting against the strong winds that blew against him. Rayen walked for miles and miles. Not making a single stop as he slowly found himself near the white mountains covered with snow and ice.

In the distance, he could see smoke coming from a place nearby and he ran to see where the smoke was rising from. Running a few miles, Rayen had stumbled upon a small cabin-like home and from the home was the smoke that he had seen. He approached the door and knocked. No response. He knocked again. No response. He knocked a third time and the door had opened and standing there facing Rayen was a hunter, who was covered from head to toe in animal skin and fur. His face could hardly be seen due to his long grayish-brown hair and facial hair.

"Who in the breezes are you?" The Hunter said.

"My name is Rayen and I am here on the journey toward the Lithiosian Castle. I was just wondering if you had anything to eat and drink. Something warm perhaps."

"We surely do. Come on right in, young man. Have yourself a seat."

Rayen entered the Hunter's home and inside Rayen noticed trophies of certain creatures and animals, they appeared to be creatures related to the planet. Rayen sat down at the wooden table and he sat in the seat next to the wood stove. The Hunter had walked into his kitchen and brought Rayen some meat and hot tea. Rayen took the meat and tea and dined on it.

"Tell me, young man. Why do you seek the Lithiosian Castle?"

"I was challenged by The Cavalier of this planet. He told me to meet him at the castle for another duel."

"So, you defeated him the first time? Hmm. That is

something very rare to hear about these days.”

The Hunter turned his head over to the other room in the home. He looked closely into the room.

“Iyera, my love, come out here and meet our guest.”

Rayen looked up and from the other room walked out Lady Iyera, the Hunter’s wife. A young woman whose beautiful countenance had caught the attention of Rayen. For he never seen a woman with such features. Her eyes were a pale blue, almost white as the Lithios sky. Her hair was black as ink. Her lips were as red as blood. Her cheekbones were seen with her strong jaw structure. She was dressed in a fur coat, but underneath it she wore a violet dress.

“Iyera, meet Rayen, an outsider of the planet. Rayen, this is Lady Iyera, my wife.”

“It is nice to gaze upon you, Rayen.”

“Pleasure to meet you, Lady Iyera.”

“This young man here is on the challenge to the castle.”

“You mean he?”

“That’s right. He defeated The Cavalier in his first battle. Decapitated the individual.”

“That is wonderful. Truly. I’ve always dreamed of meeting the man who would decapitate The Cavalier. Tell me, how was it. You know, when you chopped off his head?”

“It was necessary for the challenge. I won the first duel and I decapitated him. He placed his head back on and said to meet him here for our final duel.”

“So, he does place his head back on. I wondered about that a lot. Did he remove his helmet?”

“He did not. He basically said there would be no need in showing his face.”

A knock sounded from the front door. The Hunter stood up and opened it, walking into the home was an elderly woman, dressed in black with a fur coat and a hood over her head.

"How did the search go, ma'am?"

"Not too good." The elderly woman said. "I couldn't find what I was looking for."

"Don't worry about it. There's always another day."

"True."

She walked toward the table and Rayen stood up, giving her his seat near the wood stove and he sat in the other chair beside her. He also handed her his plate of meat and his cup of tea. She took it and nodded to him in thanks. The Hunter watched Rayen's motives toward the elderly woman and smirked.

"I sense honor within you already, young man. Tell me, where are you from?"

"I'm from Helio. The city of Tropolton to be truthful."

"Wait a minute." Iyera said. "You're one of them? One of the Abhdi Knights?"

"Yes ma'am. I am."

Iyera jumped up with excitement as she looked over at the Hunter, who smiled back at her. She turned her attention back toward Rayen.

"I have so many questions to ask you."

"I don't know if I have much time."

"When are you scheduled to meet The Cavalier at the castle?" The Hunter asked.

"On the new year. On Pesakh."

"Oh, Pesakh. I see."

"What's Pesakh?" Iyera said.

"It is the Feast Day and the start of the New Year for Those of the Avior and those who worship its Creator."

"Oh. I've never heard of such a thing."

"Really, I could teach you about it. If you were interested."

"I would be delighted to know what you know. Knight of

the Abhdi."

Rayen and Iyera smiled at one another.

"Well, here. I keep track of many dates and your new year is in three days' time. Why don't you stay here and when the day comes, you can head on out to the castle."

"Thank you, sir. I don't know how I can repay you."

"Don't worry about that. Defeating the Cavalier once and for all would be all the payment I could ask for."

Rayen stayed in the Hunter's home and spoke with Iyera concerning the Abhdi and their ways. As the night began to fall, the elderly woman entered her room of the home and went to sleep. The Hunter gave Rayen the guest room to stay in. which wasn't much but a bed, a fireplace, and a bathroom. It was enough for the young Knight. That night, the Hunter told him that he was going out to hunt for the next meal and he grabbed his shotgun and headed out into the wilderness of the night. The moon of Lithios was mich brighter and gave the Hunter an advantage during the nights.

Within the home, hours later as the elderly woman slept and Rayen laid down on the bed. He heard a knock at the door. Raising up quickly, he asks who's there and the door opens, revealing Iyera. She smiled at him as she entered the room.

"What is it?" Rayen asked.

"It's nothing." Iyera said. She stared at him deeply.

"Why are you looking at me like that?" Rayen asked. "It concerns me."

"I know you felt a connection with me during our conversation."

Rayen thought to himself, speaking to himself within his mind. He did feel a connection to Iyera and he finds her a good sight in his eyes. He looked at her and didn't know what to say back. So, he only stared.

"My husband is out hunting and it's just you and me. Make love to me, Rayen."

"Hold on. You have a husband. I could not do such a thing. It would be against my code of honor. My rank as a Knight. I cannot do that. I'm sorry."

Iyera hanged her head down, slightly saddened by Rayen's decline. Though, he placed his hand on her chin and raised her head up. He smiled at her and she did so to him.

"You have a husband. Shouldn't he be the one to make love to you."

"You speak the truth. How about a kiss."

"I'm not sure about that either."

"Just one. Please."

Rayen looked down and shook his head. Iyera continued to beg him for a kiss. He looked at her and they kissed. She smiled at him and rubbed his face with her soft hand.

"Thanks." She said leaving the room.

Rayen laid back onto the bed. Torn within himself about the act that he has committed. One side, he knows it was wrong to kiss another man's wife. The other side, however enjoyed the kiss and deeply wanted more from Iyera.

After another hour, the Hunter returned to the home with a dead Antlor laying on his sleigh. He laid the carcass next to the home and entered. He went and checked on everyone and checked on Rayen.

"How are you doing?" The Hunter asked.

"I am doing just fine, sir." Rayen said as he patted the Hunter on the back.

"What was that for?"

"For bringing me into your home. I am truly grateful."

"Don't mention it. Get some sleep, young one. You're going to need it for your quest."

The Hunter left the room and Rayen went to sleep.

The next day, the first day, Rayen had awoken from his sleep and walked out of the guest room. Sitting at the table was Iyera, who turned to him and waved slowly with a smile on her face. Rayen, smiled back as he approached the front door. Placing on his cloak, he stepped outside, out into the snowy grounds and the cold winds to see the Hunter butchering the antlor by the side of the home. The side of the home appeared to be a small barn where the Hunter would take his hunted kills and butcher them. Rayen walked to him as he watched the antlor's body hang from the side of the home.

"Oh, it seems you've awoke from your sleep." The Hunter said with a smile on his face. "How did you sleep by the way?"

"Comfortably, sir. I can't thank you enough for keeping me in your home for the time being."

"Don't mention it. You need the time and rest to prepare yourself for the Cavalier. He is a fierce one when he comes to it."

"Is there anything I can to assist you with the antlor?"

"You know how to butch beasts such as these?"

"I did some butchering myself for my brethren back home. We were trained to do it since our early youth."

"Well, come over here and help me."

Rayen walked over to the Hunter as he handed him the blade he was using for the butchering. Rayen began to butcher the antlor and he did it with excellence. The Hunter was even impressed by the way Rayen butchered the antlor. Its skin was cut off and they began to remove the internal organs from its body and drain the blood out of it. Whie they worked on the antlor, the elderly woman exited the home. She looked over at Rayen and the Hunter. Waving her hands in the air to get their attention. Rayen gazed over and seen the elderly woman, to which he tapped the Hunter on his shoulder and pointed out to her.

"The elderly woman is calling it seems." Rayen said.

The Hunter turned around and seen her standing. He knew she was about to continue her searching.

"I will be back later." The elderly woman said.

"Very well. Be careful out there."

"I surely will be."

The elderly woman walked into the wilderness and was out of sight within a split second. Rayen had watched her leave through the wilderness. Not even hearing a crack of a branch of wood not the sound of crushed snow. He wondered to himself why would the Hunter let an elderly woman enter the cold woods by herself. He stood there, squinting and gazing his eyes into the snowed forest to try and see if he could hear or see her. The Avior would only go so far in searching for her. As if there was an invisible shield blocking her from the power of the Avior.

"Don't worry about her, young man." said The Hunter. "She can take care of herself. Believe me. She roamed this land before the time I was born."

"She's been around for that long. Has she ever left the planet?"

"She said she did once. Her family went to a planet that's called Moraltis. She said the planet was filled with anger and hatred. The atmosphere was red as blood. Blackish-gray clouds covered the sky."

"I know of the planet. It is the home of the Viper Order."

"The Viper Order. You're speaking of the land where the

Dekar dwelled and remained."

"Yes sir. Myself being a Knight of the Abhdi, it is my duty to face them and defeat them. To show the Avior is more powerful and stronger than the Dekar."

"So, the whole war between Those of the Avior and Those of the Dekar began right after the Battle of Caelum took place."

"And it still continues this day. I always wondered how the universe would be if it ever ended."

"Trust me, young man, one day it will come to an end."

"How are you so sure about that?"

"Because everything within this physical world we find ourselves living in, it all will come to an end. One day."

Rayen nodded with a faint smile on his face and they continued to finish the butchering of the antlor. Lady Iyera would stand at the window, watching them do their work. She would glance at her husband and stare hard at Rayen.

To herself, she desired to know what it would be like to hold a young man such as him.

Throughout the day, Rayen sat with the Hunter and the two spoke more concerning the Avior and Dekar war. They also spoke of how the aduro weapons came into existence. Meanwhile, Iyera began preparing their supper for the day. Which was the antlor and some greens that were grown in their enclosed garden. Protected from the cold winds and the falling snow. She brought them their plates and cups of the hot tea. Which they both ate and drank. She watched them eat and drink. Showing compassion toward her husband and a lustful desire toward Rayen, who would glance at her from time to time. Showing a faint smile on his face at her. She giggled and walked into the kitchen.

From the door entered the elderly woman. She held nothing in her hands as she walked in. The Hunter looked at her, seeing if she had brought anything back with her.

"Did you find anything this time?" The Hunter asked.

"I found nothing. Absolutely nothing."

"Give it some time. You'll come across something eventually."

"I will take your word for it."

The elderly woman walked into the kitchen and grabbed herself a plate of the meat and greens. She sat down at the table close to the wood stove to keep herself warm. Rayen took off his cloak and placed it onto the elderly woman. She looked at him with compassion in her eyes.

"Thank you kindly, young man." She said gently.

"It is of my code to honor the elderly. I did what I must do."

He sat back down to his seat and finished his supper. The Hunter looked at him and so did Iyera. Hunter looked at Rayen with respect and Iyera looked at him with a fiery passion. That night when they prepared themselves for sleep. Rayen noticed the Hunter grabbing his gear to go out hunting. Rayen approached him before he left the door.

"May I ask of you a question?"

"Ask me anything."

"Why do you decide to go hunting during the night rather than the day?"

"Because the beasts of this planet tend to roam around during the night than the day. The day keeps them cool as the night gives them warmth. Plus, the moonlight helps my eyes to see them in my sights."

They both laughed as the Hunter exited the home. Rayen went into his room and laid down on the bed. Preparing to sleep. He hears a knock at the door. He answers it and its Iyera, coming to visit him again. She went over and sat on the bed.

"What are you doing?" Rayen said. "I told you I cannot."

"You can." Iyera said slowly. "You know you can do

whatever you want. Your body belongs to you does it not?"

"Look, Lady Iyera, as much as I would like to, I can't."

"I knew you would say it again. But, anyhow, you didn't bother to turn down my kiss. So, kiss me again. Two times."

"Wasn't one kiss enough the previous night?"

"For you it may have been. But for me, it was something I wanted ever since I laid my eyes on you."

Iyera took her hand and placed it onto Rayen's face. She slowly moved her hand down across his bare chest and she went lower. Rayen grabbed her hand gently, pushing it from him.

"I can't. I'm sorry."

Iyera nodded and turned away from him. Rayen felt bad for declining her and as she began to leave the room, he called back to her. She turned to him as he commanded her to approach him. She sat back onto the bed and they kissed twice.

"Thanks." Iyera said with energy in her being.

"You're welcome." said Rayen, noticing his heart was beating faster.

Iyera smiled as she left the room as Rayen laid back onto the bed. Several hours later, the Hunter made his return to the home with another kill, an Oxollo laying on the sleigh. Upon walking in, he went and checked on everyone in the home. The elderly woman was asleep as was Iyera. He went to check on Rayen and found him still awake.

"Still up are you." The Hunter said.

"For the moment."

"While you're awake, come and see my recent kill."

Rayen followed the Hunter to the door and from it Rayen could see the dead oxollo laying atop the sleigh. Rayen noticed the two horns on the side of its head and its brownish black fur hide.

"I've never seen a beast such as one before."

"Apparently, Oxollos have only been seen on this planet,

young man. It would be rare to see them anywhere else. They are related to the Oxows on Erets-Alpha. Distant cousins I believe in term of their growth."

As they entered back into the home, Rayen patted the Hunter on the back two times. The Hunter turned to Rayen, who had a smile on his face.

"What was the pats for and why are you smiling at me?"

"The pats are for your kill and the smile is for you keeping me here."

The Hunter nodded as he entered his room for sleep. Rayen returned to his room and laid down. Going asleep.

The next day, the second day, Rayen awoke from his sleep and left the room where he went outside to aid the Hunter in butchering the large oxollo. Iyera walked out of the room and spoke to Rayen, which he spoke back, gathering his cloak as he stepped outside to assist the Hunter.

When he approached him, he required his assistance in hanging the beast from the barn, for the oxollo was too large for the Hunter to hang on his own. As they worked on the beast, the elderly woman exited the home and went out into the wilderness once again. Rayen still wondered what she could be looking for.

"Don't worry about her. She'll be fine."

"What is so important for her to enter the forest on her own day after day?"

"Some family heirloom that happened to have been lost out there some time ago. She said it is of great power and could very well end the cold of this planet."

"It has that kind of power?"

"She says. She told me she hasn't seen the thing since she was of young youth. That time frame however is unknown to me if she happened to live as long as she says she has."

They continued to butcher the oxollo and within the home, Iyera continued her watching. She looked at her husband with love and she stared at Rayen with a burning lust. As if there was a fire bursting within her. Later during the day, Iyera cooked them the meat of the oxollo and a variety of greens from their garden. As they ate, the elderly woman returned to the home. Once again with nothing from the wilderness, but the frost and snow that sat on her fur coat and hood.

"Still nothing." The Hunter said.

"Still nothing." She replied as she ate and went into her room to sleep.

"Do you mind if I go out hunting with you this night?"

"Best you stay here and rest up for your bout this coming day."

Rayen nodded. "You're right."

"Get yourself some rest this time."

"I will."

The night had fell and the Hunter was off for another hunt. While the home was quiet, Iyera appeared to Rayen's room a third time and she closed the door. Sitting on the bed again. Rayen didn't know how to deal with her.

"Kiss me again, young Knight." Iyera said. "Three kisses this time."

"I can't. Weren't the two kisses enough the previous night?"

"They were. But I want more, and I desire your whole body rubbing against mine. Our bodies could warm each other."

"That cannot happen."

"Come on. My husband is gone, and the elderly woman is fast asleep. The home is quiet for the both of us to hold each other."

She placed her hand against his face and rubbed down to

his chest and went lower towards his waist. She exhaled and Rayen fought within himself. Should he turn her down or should he give into her. He took a breath and thought to himself for a moment. As her hand went lower beneath his waist, he grabbed her and kissed her. She kissed him back and laid atop him. The two began stripping of their clothes and they both were naked in the room. Rayen laid atop Iyera and kissed her from her mouth down. She moaned as he kissed her and after the kissing, she grabbed him by the throat.

"Make love to me, Rayen." She said with quick breaths.

Rayen placed himself inside of her and the two made love to each other for the night. After they had made love to one another, Iyera left the room for a moment and returned with something in her hand. It intrigued Rayen.

"What is it that you have?" He said.

"It is one of my garter belts. I figured since you'll be leaving on the morrow, you can take it with you."

"Why would I take it?"

"Because it will give you protection against The Cavalier of the Castle. During the battle against him, you'll be able to withstand all of his attacks and yours will be stronger due to the belt."

Rayen nodded as he took her garter belt. he placed it next to his tunic and cloak. She smiled at him. He smiled back.

"I thank you for the night. It was something I needed."

"No problem."

Iyera had left the room and several hours later, the Hunter returned to the home with his third kill, a Goeap. A beast smaller than the oxollo, but larger than the antlor. It possessed no horns, but its hide was covered in a white wool. The Hunter checked on everyone and last check on Rayen, who this time was fast asleep. The Hunter chuckled.

"I'll be damned. The boy went to sleep."

The Hunter placed the Goeap next to the barn and went to sleep himself. The next day, the third day, which it was the New Year and it was Pesakh. Rayen awoke and felt in his being that it was time. So, he dressed himself. Putting the garter belt in his pants pocket, beneath his tunic. He walked out of the room to tell everyone goodbye. He hugged the elderly woman, who was on her way out again and he hugged Iyera goodbye. She moved her head closely to his ear.

"The next time we see each other, we will remain together."

Rayen looked at her confusingly and slowly nodded his head as she smiled at him. He exited the home to see the Hunter butchering the goeap.

"The day has come." The Hunter said.

"It has. Thanks for everything. I owe you."

"You don't owe me. You needed shelter for the days before and I gave it to you. Do use proud and rid this land of that Cavalier."

I will do my best."

Rayen prepared to leave, but the Hunter called out to him. Rayen turned to face him and standing beside the Hunter was a white horse. A clean white. With a white mane and a white saddle and noseband. The horse neighed when Rayen turned and seen it. His eyes lit up by the beauty of the horse.

"Ride the horse on your way there." The Hunter said. "It is a long way from here."

"But, where did that horse come from?" Rayen asked.

"It came from within the barn. He usually stays in from the cold. But, I figured he could use some outside time and you can take him on your journey to the castle."

"But, how will I return the horse to you after I leave the castle?"

"Don't worry about the horse. He knows his way

throughout this land. He's been here for a very long time."

Rayen nodded and jumped up onto the horse and rode off to the distance. The Hunter watched him go as did Iyera who showed some tears as she watched Rayen ride off to the castle.

Rayen rode the horse through several valleys in their way, curved and shapeless some of the valleys were with the snowy mountains around him and some in the horizon. Rayen could look ahead and see the castle continually growing as he came closer toward it. Making a few more travels, Rayen found himself facing the castle. Which stood tall in front of Rayen. It was of a dark blue and appeared to have been built centuries before. Rayen jumped off of the horse and slowly made his way up the steps of the castle.

Rayen took slow steps and his right hand was settled on the handle of his aduroblade. He continued to walk through the castle, which echoed as he took each step and the sounds of falling ice and snow had echoed through the castle. Rayen found himself at the doors of the castle's tabernacle and he proceeded to enter. Within the tabernacle was nothing. Nothing but the cold air and snow that came through the cracked windows. The tabernacle doors closed suddenly behind Rayen. He turned back quickly, aduroblade out and glowing. Seeing no one behind him, he could feel a presence within the tabernacle with him.

"You managed to arrive, young Knight." A voice said within the tabernacle. A deep, graveling voice.

Rayen turned around and seen The Cavalier standing in the tabernacle. He locked his eyes on him and kept his aduroblade closely and tightly in his grasp.

"I have arrived and I am here to complete the challenge that you requested of me."

"Very well." The Cavalier said, pulling out another aduroaxe from his back. The axe was an exact replica of his previous one. "Let us begin."

Rayen clashed at The Cavalier and their aduro weapons collided with each other. Both fought with their skills. Rayen went for more swings and swipes to the lower body and The Cavalier went for haymakers and slams with the aduroaxe. The aduroblade and aduroaxe collided as if thunder had sounded within the tabernacle. The weapons had begun to absorb the air from the room, leaving them both gasping for air at times.

"You will not win this one!" Rayen said.

"We shall see who will overcome."

Rayen went for another swipe with the aduroblade, which The Cavalier had pushed himself back from the swipe and kicked Rayen in his leg.

"You let your anger make your decision." The Cavalier said.

Rayen stumbled as he looked up and was punched by The Cavalier in the face. Rayen fell to the ground and dropped his aduroblade, which lost its energy when it touched the cold grounds of the tabernacle. Its golden aura had disappeared, leaving only the white color to remain. The blade had become powerless. The Cavalier had won the duel.

"It appears that I have overcome this combat." The Cavalier said.

"You have defeated me." Rayen said shockingly. "How?"

Rayen stood up, ashamed of himself for his defeat and went down to his knees. He hanged his head low as The Cavalier picked up his aduroblade and held it above his neck.

"You have done what you chosen to do, young Knight."

The Cavalier went for the swing, but the aduroblade had missed Rayen's neck. Unsure of what happened, he went for another swing with the aduroblade and again it missed Rayen's neck. The Cavalier went for a third swing and this time… the blade made its mark. Though the blade did not decapitate Rayen, it only slicked the back of his neck to where a few drops of blood had come out and they dropped onto the snow. Three drops of blood.

"That was for the garter and the adultery that you have committed with my wife."

Rayen looked at The Cavalier, who was removing his helmet and behind the helmet was the Hunter of the home. The Hunter looked down at Rayen with disgust and anger. Rayen didn't have any words to say to the Hunter. He wanted to say he was sorry yet knew the Hunter would not accept his apology.

"I don't… understand." Rayen said.

"There are things in this universe that even the Elder Knights do not understand. Yet, they know their limits and they know of true honor. It appears that you do not, young Knight of the Abhdi."

"But, what of all that was at your home? The hospitality and the benevolence of you to bring me into your home?"

"I did it because I saw a young man who's never been to this planet before and the elderly woman told me of a Abhdi Knight that would make his presence known to us."

"What do you mean the elderly woman told you? How could she have known I was coming?"

"Because she is in fact a sorceress, hidden by an Ordowian enchantment for the Viper Order. They're testing out the young Knights of the Covenant. To see if you all can match them in battle before they invade your planet once more."

Rayen stood up. His heart broken and his strength faded. The Hunter hands him back his aduroblade, which he places back into its sheath. He pulls out Iyera's garter from his pocket and hands it to the Hunter. He takes it, looks at it for a brief moment and turns to Rayen.

"It is a shame that I had to send her off to an unknown planet." The Hunter said. "I'm sure she will be fine."

Rayen's heart was broken, hearing word of Iyera being sent away. He turned from the Hunter and left the castle. Making his way back to his place of origin. He entered the Helio Sor Ship, which had been covered in snow. The ship took off and after going through hyperspace, Rayen returned to Sector 333 and to Helio.

When he arrived, the residents had first begun to cheer him, that is until they seen his countenance. His armor and tunic covered in snow and dirt. His spirit could be felt by those who were around him. His spirit was broken due to his shame.

He walked into the Temple of the Avior and presented himself before the Elder Knights. He went down on his knees before them and they looked at him with a slight bit of anger.

"We know what you have committed on Lithios, Knight Rayen."

"I am sorry for my actions. My spirit tried to resist, but my flesh was too strong for me to fight."

"Be that as it may. You were warned about the distractions the Dekar would throw into your way during the quest and you didn't bother to heed them in order to accomplish the mission and keep yourself a bay from it."

"I understand."

"From this moment forward, Knight Rayen, you are hereby banished from Tropolton and into the wilderness for a period of thirty days. Within those thirty days, you are to look upon yourself and discover how you can overcome the shame you have brought onto yourself and onto your fellow brethren."

Rayen hanged his head low, no words could come from

his mouth. Only silence from his mouth and within his being. The Elder Knight approached him, commanding him to stand up and face him.

"Strip yourself of your Knighthood garments and placed your aduroblade at the door of this room."

Rayen obeyed the words that came from the Elder Knight and stripped himself of his Knighthood clothing and placed his aduroblade at the feet of the temple's doors. Rayen walked down the straight street of Tropolton, surrounded by residents. Both were disappointed and angry at Rayen's failure. Rayen didn't look back as he walked pass the gate of the city and went into the wilderness of Helio.

To correct his spiritual being and to fully understand what it means to be a Knight of the Abhdi and Those of the Avior. Within his mind, he thought, where could she be. Where could Iyera be. For Rayen had come to love her as he loves his own body.

KNIGHT RAYEN
AND THE SEARCH FOR LADY IYERA
A CHIVALRIC RESCUE OF THE *EVER WAR UNIVERSE*

719 BOC
719 YEARS DURING THE *BATTLE OF CAELUM*

I
RETURNING TO TROPOLTON

Thirty days have passed since the exile of Knight Rayen due to his actions on the planet of Lithios concerning the Hunter's wife, Lady Iyera. With the banishment having passed, Rayen made his move to return to Tropolton. During the thirty days, he roamed the wilderness of Helio. Ranging from every possible corner of the land. Encountering beasts of stature and might. Rayen fought his way through the wilderness to survive and to return to Tropolton.

Walking through the city gates, clothes torn and dirty with soil, sweat, and blood with his stench coming across the winds, Rayen returned to Tropolton. He walked down the city streets and the people of the city witnessed him, seeing his return come to pass and they let out a loud shout of joy. Many surrounded Rayne and cheered his name. They missed him and the deeds that he had done for them. Walking toward the Temple of the Avior, the Knights of the Covenant stood out and could see the crowds in the street.

"I will send the word to the Elder Knight." One Knight said to the other, returning inside the temple.

Rayen had reached the temple with the crowds standing behind him as he entered the temple doors. Walking inside, Rayen could see the Knights standing firm and he looked at them. Nodding as he approached each of them and embraced them. The Knights had missed Rayen as well. As the embracing took place, Elder Knight Iscar entered the room and witnessed the brotherly love between Rayen and the Knights.

"Knight Rayen." Elder Knight Iscar said.

Rayen turned and seen Iscar looking at him from one of the doorways. Rayen approached him and hugged him as well. Iscar was happy to see Rayen return and the Knights were even more happy and the temple was full of joy. Iscar looked at Rayen, seeing him dirty from the wilderness.

"It appears you have survived your wilderness experience."

"I understand the purpose of it, Elder and it was truly needed."

Iscar nodded and looked at the Knights.

"Leave us be for a moment." Iscar commanded as the Knights left the room of the temple.

"If I may ask, what has taken place since I've been gone?" Rayen asked.

"The usual that you are aware of. Even though, the best news is seeing you here and alive."

"Again, I know I made a terrible mistake on Lithios with the Hunter's wife and I respect the payment that I had to make."

"You are now passed that, Rayen. Meaning that you have returned to your status as an Abhdi Knight of the Covenant. Your belongings are in your chambers where we left them.”

“I thank you, Elder.”

Iscar looked closer to Rayen, seeing in his eyes something. Iscar knew what Rayen wanted to ask of him and decided on waiting to hear what it could very well be. Iscar placed his hand on Rayen’s right shoulder and nodded.

“Go and rest yourself for the night. We will speak more in the morning.”

“Yes, Elder.” Rayen said leaving for his chambers.

Inside of Rayen’s chambers, he could see the room was left the same as it was before he was exiled. he opened the closet and revealed to himself his knighthood garments and his aduroblade. Rayen held it in his hands and removed the sheath from the blade, looking as its white and gold glowing power and might. Placing it back into its sheath, Rayen had eaten and later washed himself during the night before heading to sleep. During the night in his sleep, Rayen dreamt of Lady Iyera being moved around from planet to planet. Nation to nation and sector to sector. He awoke as the sun arose in the city and he went down to see Iscar. Iscar walked down the hall and could see Rayen walking toward him and he knew it was something of importance by the way Rayen walked down the hall in haste.

“Elder, I need to speak to you concerning a matter.”

“Speak it.”

“It is about Lady Iyera. Now, I know that she was the Hunter’s wife and I laid with her. Thus committing adultery. Before I returned, the Hunter told me that he sent her away before we fought in the Lithiosian Castle and that she was moved to another planet in the sectors like a harlot. I do have to ask of you, does my action make her my wife?”

Iscar nodded his head and looked into Rayen’s eyes, seeing that he wanted the truth and the genuine answer to such a question.

"Knight Rayen, she is your wife. Now, I understand there is something else you wished to ask of me and I am sure of what it is."

"I had a dream and I saw her being moved around the sectors and nations. She is in turmoil and distress and I want to go out there and find her. Bring her here to live with me as my wife."

Iscar nodded, taking in the words that Rayen has spoken to him. Iscar discerned Rayen's spirit and could see that he wasn't in the same mindset as when he left before. Iscah seen a change in Rayen and it was of a mature spirit.

"You desire to bring her here and to live with you? She must understand that she has to conform to our laws, our statures, and our commandments if she intends on returning with you to remain here as your wife."

"Yes, Elder. I desire to find her and to bring her here with me. After all, she is my responsibility now."

"Very well, Knight Rayen. I grant you this task that you have spoken of. But, be on your guard. Keep the guard stronger than what you had done before."

Rayen hugged Iscar with joy.

"I will see to it that she understands the terms before making the move."

"See that she makes the choice and guard your heart with all diligence."

Rayen prepared himself inside of his chamber as he dressed in his Knight garments and held his aduroblade on his side. He walked out of the temple where the people could see him and they questioned in themselves where was Rayen going. He entered one of the Helio-Sor ships and prepared it for takeoff.

"It's been a while since I've flown one of these."

The ship hovered in the air and took off with a blast of wind into the air and vanished into the sky. Rayen was now in stellar space and his search for Lady Iyera had begun.

35

II
CITY OF IERICHO

Flying through stellar space across Sector 333, Rayen headed towards Erets-Alpha to find information of Iyera's possible whereabouts. Though, he was uncertain as to what he may discover upon entering the planet's atmosphere and what city she could be residing in throughout Erets-Alpha. Rayen had no other information on himself besides the minor details given to him by the Hunter back on Lithios and the dream he had during the night. Rayen could remember the locations in the dream and decided to use it as the focus of his search. Which leads Rayen to Erets-Alpha.

Entering the circular planet's atmosphere and coming down to the surface, Rayen found himself on the eastern side of the planet. Landing on the dirt grounds, Rayen exited the ship and found a sign to his right as he glanced around the location. Rayen approached the sign, which appeared to have been standing there forages, rusting away due to the sun and the excess of time. Rayen could comprehend the language written on the sign.

"Iericho." He said.

From nearby came three men who was wanderers of the land. They were dirty, smelly, and dressed in black clad leather with ponchos covering them. From a quick point of view they saw the ship and they saw Rayen standing outside of it looking at the sign. The wanderers sought out a plan and made themselves known to Rayen.

"Young man, could you assist us in a favor." One

wanderer spoke.

"I don't know who you are." Rayen stated, measuring them and himself. "But, I can say you look like Star Raiders to me."

"Funny. Star Raiders."

"Who are you men?"

"Why do you need to know? Better yet, listen. Me and my friends just need a ride out of this planet and to somewhere else. Somewhere better."

"Why don't you go and buy yourselves a ship. Fly yourselves out of here with no problems."

"That's the thing. We don't see ships of your kind here often. By the look of it, I would say it belongs to those Knights over on Helio."

"It's one of theirs." The other wanderer yelled. "He's one of those Knights. Look at his tunic."

The wanderers looked at Rayen's tunic, seeing the gold crest on his white tunic. The wanderers held up their ranges and pointed them at Rayen. The lead wanderer smiled and let out a loud laugh.

"I will tell you this, young one. Give us this ship and you can go on being free."

"I will not give you the ship and it appears that the three of you won't be going anywhere."

"What's that supposed to mean?"

Rayen nodded and pulled out his aduroblade and swiped the wanderers hands from their arms in a quick pace. The wanderers yelled in pain as they now only possess one hand each. Rayen took the aduroblade and killed them.

Placing the blade back into its sheath, Rayen looked around the sandy grounds to see if anyone else was walking about the land. No one is seen nor found in Rayen's sights.

From the back of the ship ejected a land-veho which

Rayen used to travel on the grounds of the planet with much haste rather than having to walk. Riding the veho through the landscape and seeing nothing but sandy grounds and tall trees covered with green and brown leaves, Rayen could see a city ahead and he knew it had to be Iericho as the sign had said.

Coming upon the city, Rayen could see that it was inhabited with many enashians. They range from different shades of hue and are a mixed multitude of people.

The residents of the city turned their focus on Rayen as he entered through the city gates. He stopped, to where an elderly man dressed in a brown tunic with a white coat approached him from the side. The elderly man saw the Knights' crest on Rayen's tunic and pointed with both fear and honor.

"You're not from around here."

"I am not. But, I come with a purpose."

"Such as?"

"Have any of you seen a woman come here recently. She has jet black hair, her skin is pale, almost as white as snow, and she has a beautiful countenance."

"I may have seen somewhere of that description, young one."

"Do you know if she's here by any chance?"

"You'll have to take that up with the king of the land."

"Where is he?"

The elderly man pointed toward the pyramidal structure that sat near the middle of the city. Rayen nodded to the man and kept moving. The elderly man went about his business as other residents stared at Rayen riding through the city. Once Rayen reached the structure that stood about forty feet in height and made with mud bricks of the land. Rayen walked its steps toward the entrance. The doors had opened and Rayen found himself entering the structure. Sitting in front of him were two guards and further out sat the king of the city. The King of Iericho. Rayen stood in front of him and the King measured Rayen greatly. Even the guards stared at Rayen. They could sense something about him and it was different from anything near the city. They could tell he was from another place from his garments, armor, and aduroblade.

"Who are you and why have you come to my city?"

"I am Rayen Grake of the Knights of the Covenant. I have come here to this planet and to your city to ask of some information that I require."

"What kind of information?"

"I seek a woman that may have been brought here sometime ago. Her name is Lady Iyera. She was once a resident of the planet Lithios before her husband sent her away. Where he sent her, I am not sure. But, this place is where I had to start the search."

The King of Iericho nodded his head. Taking in every word that Rayen had spoken to him. He meditated for a few seconds before coming up with a response.

"You come to my city. The city of Iericho ask of a missing woman?"

"Yes, King of Iericho."

"Tell me, what is the reason for your search of this Lithiosian woman? You said her husband sent her away and yet, it is you who's searching for her. Why?"

"She is now my wife and I must reclaim her."

"Oh. I see now. Fitting how such actions would take place in my city. The neighboring cities wouldn't dare accept such actions being committed unless they were of a low respect."

"I have read about the cities of *Sedom* and *Amorah* and what they have become."

"Nothing but ash and sulfur they are. Because of their actions in the ancient days. From what I could learn, only a man and his daughters survived the catastrophe."

"So, King of Iericho, I ask of you humbly, do you have any information regarding Lady Iyera and her whereabouts?"

The King stood up from his throne and walked down its stairs toward Rayen on the floor. The King stopped and faced Rayen eye to eye. He discerned Rayen's spirit and could see a far stronger power from within him. The King nodded with a smile.

"I can tell you that she was here some days ago. But, she was moved away."

"Moved where?" Rayen asked.

"From what I was told, they took her to the sector, Star 114 to the moon called Quortos. They said it could hold habitable life and they decided to take her there."

"Who is them?"

"They were dressed in Raider apparel. Although, on their chests they wore the crest of the Viper Order. Other than what I have told you, I do not know."

Rayen extended his arm toward the King of Iericho.

"Thank you for your information."

"I do what I can to assists those in need of greater details. After all, I am a king."

They shook arms and Rayen left the structure of the King and went atop the veho and left the city of Iericho, returning to the Sor ship. Upon making his return to the ship, Rayen opened up the map from within and directed a path toward the sector Star 114 to find the moon Quortos. Locked on the target, the ship hovered and bolted out of Erets-Alpha like a lightning bolt.

III
THE HABITABLE MOON

Flying over Star 114, Rayen looked out of the ship's window and seen Quortos. Preparing to enter into the moon's atmosphere, Rayen went toward the moon and as soon as the ship made impact with the atmosphere, all sight was covered by the moon's clouds. Rayen moved the ship through the clouds smoothly and from the clouds came the landscape, which looked like a jungle moon. Trees and fields and mountains and lakes covering the grounds of Quortos with the fowls of the air flying over and above. Rayen was astounded by the beautiful sight of the moon.

"Look at this place."

Rayen scouted the landscape, flying the ship low. He thought of where would someone reside on the moon and he first looked toward the trees, but there were no structures built upon the trees. He turned to the fields and he seen no house or tents. He looked over to the lakes and there were no structures built and he turned the ship and gazed at the mountains. He looked closer and could see what appeared to be an entrance into a cave.

"There. That is where I will search."

Rayen made his plan and landed the ship on the grounds in front of the mountains. He walked up the ridges of the mountain toward the proposed cave entrance and found his way inside. Within the cave itself was some ancient enashian writing on the walls and on the grounds. Rayen searched the cavern and found nothing, but as he was leaving he stepped on something buried underneath the dirt of the mountain. Rayen dug into the dirt with his hands and found a buried map.

On the map were several planets in different sectors. Rayen couldn't comprehend the writing on the map for it was not of his native tongue. Though, Rayen knew where he could have the map translated and he would make his decisions afterwards. Just as Rayen was preparing to leave the moon, thumping sounds were heard coming from the trees. Rayen stopped and looked around to see what could be the cause and from the tall trees of the ground appeared an Asper, one of the red breed and it stood tall over Rayen as it made Rayen feel as if he was a grasshopper in his own sight. The gorilla-like beast roared at Rayen as he ran for the ship and entered.

"This is not good."

The ship hovered and flew off with the asper chasing him through the fields and the trees. Rayen dodged the trees that were in his way with the asper knocking them down from behind. Rayen found himself entering a field covered by trees and the asper jumped in front of the ship and started pounding its fists into the ground. The asper beat its chest and roared. Rayen was set to fire at the beast and from the trees bolted out a Wilderness Masmodon, who's large tusks snatched the asper and drove it into the trees behind Rayen's ship. Rayen watched as the asper and the masmodon fought each other with both beasts fighting to the death. The apser was trying to claw its way through the thick brown fur of the masmodon. The masmodon used its tusk to trip the asper and began stomping the gorilla beast into the ground. Rayen escaped the sight and entered into the sky where he could only hear the sound of the asper's screeching roar and the masmodon's trumpet horn.

After exiting the moon of Quortos, Rayen took a

moment to gaze upon the map once more and examined the language it was written in. Rayen took some time to meditate on the language and made the decision to travel to the planet where that language was dominant. Returning to Sector 333, Rayen passed by the neighboring planet, even Helio and made his trip toward the planet of Endor, the home of the Regnum Trinitas religion and the base for the Regnum Caelorum and the mountain of Conscendo Sceleratus. Rayen knew he had to speak with the king of the planet, which is a descendant of the Ard family

<u>IV</u>
THE KINGDOM OF ARD

Flying through Sector 333, Rayen looked ahead and seen Endor, the home of the Ard Family. He made his way toward the planet, which shined with a light blue, a dark blue, and white colors. Rayen entered the atmosphere of Endor and he could see the clouds were covered in ice and the grounds beneath him were of rock and ice. Rayen was reminded of Lithios when he seen the grounds of Endor. He flew over the mountains of Endor and found in front of him a kingdom. The kingdom was the land of the Ard Family and their primary residence.

Rayen landed the ship in the other circle of the kingdom and exited. Taking a small walk from the ship to the kingdom, Rayen stood in front of a large gate. The gate is known and called by many the Gate of Regnum. It stood over fifteen feet in height and its width was nearly as wide as Rayen's ship. Made from the glacier minerals of the planet itself. Rayen stood still.

"Is anyone here?" Rayen yelled.

From the other end of the Gate appeared the Regnum Knights, known as the Ard-Knights of Endor. Dressed in white and blue armor. Their faces were covered by their helmets that only revealed their eyes. They carried swords with them and detailed onto their white tunic were the emblem of the Ard Family. The Ard-knights faced Rayen from the other side of the Gate.

"Speak of your name and your purpose here."

"I am Rayen Grake of the Knights of the Ancient Covenant. I have come to speak with your king in a particular search. I require his assistance in deciphering."

They paused themselves for a brief moment. Holding up their swords. taking several steps back from the Gate and standing against the walls. Rayen watched as they moved themselves to the side and the Gate opened. It opened brightly and it shined as it opened. Rayen proceeded to walk through and he did. After entering through the Gate, the Ard-knights stood on Rayen's sides and escorted him into the Kingdom of Ard.

Walking through the kingdom, Rayen seen the residents of the kingdom and how they were dressed. Almost as the same as those back on Helio, but with a slight twist and difference. Nearing the location of the king, called and known to the sectors as the Regnum Caelorum, Rayen seen three statues made from both stone and ice. The statues were of the three gods of Endor, primarily of the Regnum Trinitas. In order the statues were, All-Father Ard, Son-Ard, and Spirit of Ard. Reaching back into the ancient days when the planet of Endor was filled with enashians. Rayen looked away from the statues and inside himself he felt shame for the people of Endor. For they know not what they are doing to themselves in the grand scheme of the universe.

The doors of the Regnum Caelorum opened up and the Ard-knights allowed Rayen to enter and they continued to follow. The doors shut and Rayen measured the interior of the structured building. The building was of ancient age and it held artifacts dating back to the beginning of the Battle of

Caelum to the Cavalier Civil War. From one of the corridor doors appeared a young man. He had blonde hair and blue eyes. He wore the garments and coat of the family of Ard and he had a crown of ice on his head. He is the current King of Endor named Carthadus-Ard. The son of the late Siegfried-Ard, the legendary Endorian king.

"Now, what is this?" Carthadus said.

"This man claims to be one of the Covenant Knights, your majesty."

"I can tell you that he is, soldier. Leave us."

The Ard-knights bowed before Carthadus and exited the building. Leaving the large room only to Rayen and Carthadus. Carthadus greeted Rayen with a big hug and full of joy.

"It is good to see another one of you again."

"I have only heard of the things that the Knights and your forefathers have achieved together."

"Well, since you're here, I can tell you more about them. But, I have to ask, what brings you here on this day?"

"I have something that requires your assistance. For I cannot read your language."

"What is it?"

Rayen reached into his pockets and showed Carthadus the map he found on Quortos. Carthadus gazed at the map and could see the writings were Endorian and he nodded with a smile. He looked at Rayen and waved the map.

"I can help you with this. Follow me."

Rayen followed the Ard-King of Endor down the corridor. Carthadus spoke to him about the history between the Knights and the kings of Endor before him. Rayen only had little knowledge about the events and he could only remember them if they were mentioned in great detail. For most of the history took place before his birth.

"Funny, how my father and his fathers before him aligned with the Knights to face off the threats that came before them in the ancient days."

"Your father, Siegfried-Ard. I have heard in the history books that he defeated the dragon called Blath the Wicked during the Cavalier Civil War."

"As a matter of fact, he did. During those times, my father was young and Blath was ravaging the sectors with terror. Most of the Endor Council refused to fight the dragon, but my father decided to take on the dragon by himself. So, when Blath had taken over this kingdom for himself and resided at the mountain called Conscendo Sceleratus, my father went over to the mountain and faced the dragon."

"How did he fair against Blath?"

"He lost several times before gaining the strength and killing the beast with the Carus Sword. Afterwards, my father kept the sword by his side at all times and only used that sword when he was in battle."

"Did you bury the sword with your father?"

"I will show you his resting place and it will make things much clearer to you."

Carthadus led Rayen down another corridor. This corridor went outside and as they walked Carthadus pointed to his right and Rayen looked and could see a mountain. The mountain was covered in snow and clouds. Rayen could also see some remnants of ancient statues on the mountain. Statues of the ancient Ard-Kings carved in the mountain itself.

"That mountain is Conscendo Sceleratus. The mountain where Blath landed and resided."

Walking past the corridor, Carthadus opened another door and this door lead into a room. The room was sealed shut from outside and within the room were bodies. The bodies of the kings of old. Rayen entered the room and seen the coffins of the Ard-Kings who came before Carthadus.

"This is the Sleeping Room of Kings." Carthadus said. "This is the final place where they remain."

"So, every king that has come before you lies within this very room?"

"Every Ard-King there ever was. Come and I will show you my father's resting place."

Rayen followed Carthadus deeper into the room and through there they passed by many of the ancient kings of the past. They passed by the ice-built tombs of *Ingelram-Ard, Bertramus-Ard, Emaldus-Ard, Ancelmus-Ard, Altor-Ard,* and from them Carthadus stopped and faced the coffin of his father. Rayen looked and could see the body of Siegfried-Ard. Whose body was very well-preserved. No signs of decomposing and he still looked the same when he was alive. His long white hair remained and he wore his war armor of Endor.

"Here he is, Rayen."

"The man who killed Blath the Wicked."

Carthadus pointed up above the coffin toward an object and Rayen could see it. The object was the Carus Sword and it sat over Siegfried-Ard's coffin. The sword made of the ice of the mountain and the metal of Endor. Rayen took in what he was witnessing and he couldn't believe it himself. Seeing the Carus Sword in his presence. A sword that only few have gazed their eyes on and others believe to be a myth.

"The sword's been in here since his death?"

"Ever since. It has not been moved nor used since his final war against the Viper Order."

"May I ask of his age?"

"He was five hundred years old. He told me when he would die before it came to pass and he was right. Funny enough, he lived longer than most of the kings before his time. Lived one hundred years longer than his father.”

Rayen could see the emotion coming from Carthadus as he looked at his father’s body in the ice coffin. Rayen nodded and comforted Carthadus before they left the room. Both took one look back at Siegfried’s coffin and the Carus Sword before the door closed and locked. They continued walking until they reach Carthadus’ office room and inside the room, Carthadus started to decipher the language of the map. Rayen looked at the office and seen the paintings of the Ard-Kings and their victories. One painting featured Siegfried aligned with a Knight of the Covenant in battle against the Viper Order on Thran.

“That’s Elder Iscar.” Rayen said pointing.

“You know of him I see.”

“I do. I know him very well.”

“I can tell by your voice that he’s still alive and that is something to behold.”

“He’s younger on the painting. Though, I will behold that as you‘ve said.”

Carthadus finished deciphering the language and presented to Rayen its written translation on a scroll. Rayen held the scroll and read. What he read detailed Lady Iyera’s movements. From Lithios to Erets-Alpha to Quortos to two unknown planets. The planets couldn’t be deciphered. Rayen understood it and thanked Carthadus for his help.

“Tell me if you may, who is this lady Iyera you’re searching for?”

“She is my wife. My first wife.”

“And she was taken from you I’m guessing?”

“In a matter. She was and she wasn’t. A mistake I had done made her my wife and now I must live by the rules of being a husband.”

"I can comprehend your words. I have yet to find a wife, but I know that I must to insure the continuation of the Ard Family. Maybe someday, our sons will meet and aligned just as our forefathers did."

"May that be so."

Rayen and Carthadus extended arms and greeted. Rayen prepared to leave and Carthadus stopped him before he exited the Gate of Regnum.

"If I hear of any news concerning your wife, I will contact you and send you the message."

"I appreciate it, Carthadus.'

"It's what our forefathers done for each other."

Rayen exited the gate and it closed. Carthadus returned to the Regnum Caelorum as Rayen entered the ship and flew out of the planet of Endor. While trying to figure out the two planets, Rayen discovered his aduroblade had been damaged. Believing it to have occurred back on Quortos when invading the asper. Making a decsion that may delay his search for Iyera, Rayen took the attempt and traveled back to sector Star 114. Passing by Quortos, Rayen made his landing set for the planet of Sudravor. The home planet of the dwarves.

<h1 style="text-align:center"><u>V</u>
THE DWARVES OF SUDRAVOR</h1>

Rayen approached the planet of Sudravor and he can immediately see the smoke coming from the grounds of the planet. Entering the atmosphere, Rayen could see the flames and the large clouds of smoke around him. Where Rayen was landing the ship was in front of a mining section of the planet. The section where the dwarves dig in front of a large statue made of rock in honor of The Mining One, the Sudravorian god.

The dwarves witnessed the landing of the ship and Rayen exited, confronting them about his matters. The dwarves themselves were dressed in iron-clad armor and helmets of silver and of black. The dwarves gazed and measured their eyes at Rayen's garments and some kneeled before him as others did not. Rayen stopped walking as he witnessed some of the dwarves bowing down to him.

"There's no need for you to be bowing to me. Please, stand yourselves up."

From one of the mining caverns walked out an elder dwarf. He stood at about five feet in height and his beard almost touched the ground as did his long gray and black hair. He wore armor similar to the other dwarves, but wore a brown cloak on his back. The dwarf approached Rayen.

"It has been sometime since a Knight of the Covenant made themselves known to our home once again."

"I come here with a purpose and it requires your assistance."

"Then show me what it is you have brought to us."

Rayen pulled out his aduroblade and it was cracked in the center and on its corners. The glowing energy of the blade was flashing and fading away. The dwarf held the blade and measured it. Signaling for the other dwarves to come near him and he handed them the aduroblade, which they took to one of the nearby shacks for repair.

"Follow me, Knight." The elder dwarf said.

Rayen followed the dwarf to the shack as he seen the other dwarves continuing their mining work in the caverns and some where even building other aduroblades. Blades not yet seen by the outsiders of Sudravor.

"No need to worry yourself over receiving a new blade, boy. We'll have yours fixed up in a matter of time and you can return about your business."

"I thank you for your help."

"Though, tell me, why you chose to gain our help rather than the Orchs on Dagobar?"

"Truth be told, your planet was nearest on my radar and in my direction. If I were on the other ends, Dagobar would've been the option that I would've taken."

"Those odds work in your favor, Knight of the Covenant." The elder dwarf declared nodding. "But, however, we will fix it up and it will be as it was when you first received it. It will look reborn and renewed."

Rayen nodded to the elder dwarf in appreciation and assistance. The dwarves went to work on Rayen's aduroblade and he sat on the outside of the shack, watching the other dwarves work on the caverns and on the other objects they were building. He could see the dwarves had salvaged some tech from the Viper Order ranging from fragments of their Eglah ships to rain shocker armor, even a few of the dwarves were wearing the rainshocker breastplates. Rayen chuckled at the sight of it.

The elder dwarf appeared before Rayen and handed him his aduroblade. Rayen looked at it and it was renewed. The cracks were gone and the blade had a brighter glow to it than it did before. Rayen thanked the dwarves fro their help and they responded back with a beat to their chest and a nod. Rayen had told the dwarves to remember the Knights of the Covenant will always be allies with the dwarves when the circumstances approve of it. They agreed to the matter and returned to their work.

Rayen returned to the ship and inside was a message from Carthadus. Rayen answered the message and Carthadus appeared before him in the form of a hologram.

"Rayen, I have news concerning your wife, Iyera."

"What have you found?"

"First off, I have discovered the two unknown planets on the map. They are both Ordow and Sinstor."

"Then, I should head over to them both."

"Hold on for just a second, Rayen."

"What else is there?"

"Don't bother going over to Ordow. She isn't there any longer."

"Which leaves only Sinstor."

"She was sent there a few days ago and is kept as a serving girl and a possible mistress to the Pharao. Are you sure about confronting him in his own kingdom? You know that Sinstor isn't the same since its been underneath the new rule of the Second Dynastic Magocracy."

"I have no other choice to take, Carthadus. I thank you for this news and I am heading for Sinstor."

"Very well. Take care of yourself when you get there, Brother Knight."

"I will do so."

Rayen turned on the ship and left the planet of Sudravor with the dwarves watching the ship fly in the air and vanish from their eyesight. Rayen reentered stellar space and charted a trail toward the sector of Star 895, which held the planet Sinstor as well as the Viper Order planet of Moraltis. The ship took off on the trail, making a quick arrival for Sinstor.

VI
DIVINITY AGAINST MAGIC

The ship flew at hyper speed on the trail charted by Rayen and instantly the ship stopped and in front of Rayen was Sinstor. The planet looked like a desert planet with fields of grass and trees. Rayen went ahead toward the planet and as he came closer he could feel its magic surrounding the planet. Both from the outside and from inside. The ship moved with such speed that it caused a sonic boom in the sky after making its entrance into the atmosphere. From the grounds in the Sinstorian capital city of Misrayim, the residents looked up at the sky, seeing the Helio Sor ship coming near them. The Sinstorian soldiers immediately ran into the temple room of the Pharao.

"Pharao, we have urgent news to tell you."

Inside the temple room and sitting on the throne was Pharao Sebek-Em-Of and sitting next to him in a similar seat was his son, Prince Amran-Em-Of. The future Pharao of Sinstor. Both were dressed in white garments with gold and jewels across their necks and they both wore rings of different minerals on their fingers. Pharao's crown was also long and white with golden decorated around it. They both seen the soldiers coming in at great pace from the outside and were intrigued to know about their urgency.

"Speak of your news." Pharao demanded.

"A Helio Sor ship has just bolted from the sky and is

making its way here to Misrayim. We believe it to be a Knight of the Covenant, Great Pharao.”

“I am aware of such a possibility.” Pharao said. “When he exits his ship, bring him here to my presence. I know why he’s here and what he’s come for.”

“Yes, Great Pharao.”

The soldiers ran out of the temple room and from the left side of Pharao appeared an elderly woman. The same woman that was in Lithios with the Hunter and Iyera. Coming behind her were the serving girls and one of them was Iyera herself. Dressed in the serving clothes of the Sinstorians. Her hair decked in little gold and she wore a white garment that was similar to a dress and she wore sandals. She sat on the stairs next to Pharao.

“It appears that he has come, my lady.” Pharao said to the elderly woman.

“It was bound to happen soon. When he gets here, you already know what to make of him.”

Outside, Rayen flew the ship passed the Pyramids of Xanthou and made his landing not too far from the temple rooms. Rayen exited the ship in haste and grabbed his aduroblade. Making his way toward the temple, he was surrounded by Sinstorian soldiers, armed with sickles, spears, and swords. Rayen kept his guard while gazing at them. One man standing amongst ten.

“Think about this before making your moves.” Rayen said.

“We have not come to harm you, Knight.” A soldier said. “We are here to escort you to the Great Pharao. He demands your presence immediately.”

Rayen took in the words of the soldiers and slowly

placed his adorable into its sheath and followed the soldiers toward the temple room. As they walked, Rayen looked over at the Yeor Waterlands and from them he could see the Yeor Dragons running in and out of the water, snatching the stranded oxow and dragging them into the water. They ran on all fours and their bodies were scaly and their jaws were narrow and long with sharp teeth.

They approached the temple room and the doors opened. The first thing Rayen noticed were the statues of the Sinstorian gods and the ancient Pharaos of the past. Rayen also noticed several Eglah aeronauts walking on about in the temple rooms. Noting that the Viper Order have made their presence there. They escorted Rayen into the throne room where Pharao was waiting for him.

The throne room doors had opened and the soldiers allowed Rayen to enter on his own. When he entered, his eyes locked onto Pharao and sitting at Pharao's feet was Iyera. Rayen went to run for her, but was stopped by the soldiers on Pharao's command. Iyera began to tear up, seeing Rayen once again. Rayen was being held back by the soldiers as the Pharao looked at him. Rayen also spotted the elderly woman and she was staring at him, laughing.

"So, you are the one they told me that was coming. You want this woman back don't you?"

"She is my wife and she belongs with me."

"That I can understand. But, you didn't think that I would just hand her over to you and let you go about your lives."

"What do you want from me?"

"Simple. If you love her as much as your actions have shown this day, you will have no problem fighting for her."

"Why would I have to fight for your amusement or that witch?"

"It's not for my amusement, boy. I want to see if you've truly the man you've say you've become. Fight my chosen warrior. Defeat him and you can have your wife back. Be defeated and you will remain at my service and you will serve the Mystical Ones for all of your days."

Rayen nodded and Pharao commanded his soldiers to stand back from Rayen and they did. Giving him room. Rayen looked at them and around the room, trying to find out who he will have to fight against. The elderly woman also looked around for his opponent and she approached Pharao.

"Who will you place against him? It must be someone of great power. A power similar to mine and similar to the Viper Order."

"What are you suggesting?"

"Let him face me and I will deal with him quickly."

"No. He's a man and he will face a man."

"Then, who do you have in mind? You're not going to fight him yourself are you?"

Pharao turned to his right, looking at his son. Amran seen his father gazing toward him as he pointed to Rayen.

"Go, my son. Face him and defeat him. Make him a slave to Sinstor and he may very well be your servant when you become Pharao."

Amran stood from the seat and walked down the stairs onto the floor, facing Rayen. One of the serving girls approached Amran with a weapon and he held it and the weapon glowed a bluish hue and was made of solid gold. The weapon was an aduroaxe and staff hybrid. Rayen was astonished by the weapon and nodded at its beauty. He went and raised up his aduroblade, which glowed with a golden energy covering the white blade.

"Let the battle commence!" Pharao yelled.

The Prince of Sinstor bolted toward Rayen with the

aduroaxe-staff and Rayen blocked the twirling attacks with the aduroblade. Rayen went to kick Amran in the legs, but Amran jumped up before Rayen's foot made contact. Both men clashed their weapons together, causing a small boom of thunder to echo throughout the throne room. Rayen and Amran fought with their strength, shoving against one another in battle. Rayen used his elbow to hit Amran in the forehead and tripped him with his leg. Amran kicked himself up and twirled the aduroaxe/staff and swiped it across Rayen's chest, cutting his tunic. Iyera panicked for a split second as Amran signaled for Rayen to attack and Rayen ran for him with the aduroblade. Rayen took the butt of the blade and jammed it into Amran's chest and tackled him onto the golden floor.

"I hope your son is as skillful as you believe him to be." The elderly woman said.

"Don't worry. He has a lot of skills outside of fighting. My son will become a fine Pharao."

Amran continued to twirl the aduroaxe/staff against Rayen, who kept blocking the attacks with the aduroblade. Rayen fought back with swipes and slashes, one slash cut Amran's arm and he started to bleed from the slash and they both fought harder against each other in front of those in the room. Pharao was awaiting for Amran to defeat Rayen and be done with him.

"There will be no exodus this time!" Sebek yelled. "Not during my reign!"

While they fought, the Eglah Aeronauts entered the room and witnessed the battle. Rayen blocked another attack from Amran and swiped the aduroblade against the aduroaxe/staff, knocking it out of Amran's hands. Rayen kicked him in his chest and stood over him with the aduroblade held above his throat.

"What is this!" Pharao yelled in anger. "What has happened here?!"

"Your son has lost." Rayen said, looking at Pharao. "That is what has happened here."

"Go ahead then, Knight of the Covenant. Finish him off and take your prize."

Rayen looked down at Amran on the ground. He thought about lodging the blade into his throat and killing the young Prince. But, he later thought what would be the purpose and chose not to kill the Prince of Sinstor. Rayen stood away from Amran and helped him off the floor and they stood side by side. Rayen grabbed Amran's weapon and handed it back to him.

"I will not kill your son, Pharao." Rayen said. "Judging by the way he fights, I sense a great form of honor within him. He will become a more powerful Pharao than you will ever become."

"Your words mean little to me, boy. Go ahead and take your wife. Leave my kingdom and my planet."

Pharao allowed Iyera to run down to Rayen and she did. Rayen ran toward her and they embraced each other with a kiss and a long hug. Iyera cried as Rayen held her. Amran walked past them and could see the love they had for one another. He nodded and returned to his seat on the throne as the serving girls managed his bleeding arm. The elderly woman ran off with the Eglah Aeronauts.

"Let's go home." Rayen said with a smile.

They left the temple room, returning to the ship and as they walked outside, above them flew past two Eglahs and inside one of them was the elderly woman sitting in the passenger seat.

"Who is she?" Iyera asked.

"She is the cause for most of your troubles and mine."

They entered the ship and left the planet of Sinstor. Meanwhile, inside the temple rooms, Amran sat by himself, mediating on the words that Rayen spoke concerning him and his future as Pharao.

VII
REUNITED IN TROPOLTON

Rayen and Iyera were making their way to Helio and to return to Tropolton. Inside the ship, the two were happy to see each other again. Rayen sat down, watching the planet of Helio coming up in front of them. He smiled at the sight of it and Iyera sat close to him.

"Tell me, why didn't you kill him?"

"Because the Avior told me not to. There's a future for that Prince and it will affect a lot of us."

"I see."

They approached Helio and the ship entered into the atmosphere and as they came close to landing in Tropolton, the Knights were standing outside and could see the ship coming. They knew it was Rayen and they went inside to inform Elder Knight Iscar about Rayen's return. The ship could be seen by all who were in the city and Iscar walked outside as the ship made its landing. Rayen and Iyera exited the ship to see Iscar and the Knights standing there waiting for him.

"You've returned." Iscar said, hugging Rayen.

'I have and not alone."

Iscar looked and seen Iyera standing next to Rayen.

"So, you are the Lady Iyera." Iscar greeted. "I take it she will be residing here for the rest of her days."

"I learned a valuable lesson, sir." Iyera said to Iscar. "I know that I was the cause to Rayen's mishap, but not anymore."

Iscar nodded and smiled.

"Come then, let us eat and drink and discuss your plans for the future to come."

Rayen and Iyera followed Iscar and the Knights into the temple as the residents of the city cheered them on. A few days after, Rayen and Iyera chose to have a formal marriage and they did and it was held by Iscar himself. They were formally married in a ceremony overseen by The High One and Iyera stayed with Rayen in his chambers of the city.

Sometime later, Rayen came to Iscar in the temple.

"Elder, I have something to ask you."

"Ask."

"In my search for Iyera, I made a travel to Endor and I spoke with their current king. He showed me around his kingdom and there I seen a painting. It was of Siegfried-Ard and one of us on the battlefield of Thran fighting the Viper Order. I'm not understanding it."

"Why do you not understand it?"

"The Covenant Knight resembled you. In your youth."

Iscar nodded and placed his hand on Rayen's shoulder.

"There are things I have not told you and neither have I told the Knights regarding those events."

"So, you were there? You fought alongside Siegfried-Ard?"

"We fought beside each other many times."

"But, how?"

"Because, I am older than most know me to be. I was born five years before Siegfried-Ard and that currently makes me five hundred and forty one years old."

Rayen nodded.

"I will tell you more in the times to come, my son. You

will know much more.”

YABEL,
THE KNIGHT OF THE SALVATION
A CHIVALRIC JOURNEY OF THE *EVER WAR UNIVERSE*

695 BOC
695 YEARS DURING THE *BATTLE OF CAELUM*

I
THE WANDERING KNIGHT

In the parts of stellar space comes a ship. A ship which is beaten down and rugged. Kicking itself to continue its flight through the flowing of space. The ship is approaching a planet. The planet glows with a golden hue and is covered in lush green. The planet the ship is heading for is Helio. The home of the Knights of the Covenant. The ship inches closer and bursts itself through the planet's atmosphere, heading for a crash into the wilderness. The ship jolts and kicks, smashing into trees and finally crashes onto the ground. The ship door opens and out comes a man, covered in silver armor from head to toe. He appeared to be a knight and his armor was beaten with dents, cuts, and drops of blood. He appeared to have been in a battle before crashing.

"Is this the place?" He said to himself, gazing around the trees and bushes that circled him and his fallen ship.

The knight climbed up one of the tall trees of the wilderness and found himself able to see afar off from where he was located. In the distant, he could see a city. The city is Tropolton and in the middle of the city is the Temple of the Avior, glowing brightly. The knight nodded.

"That's the place." He said. "They must be inside those walls."

The knight grabbed whatever was left of his gear and

walked away from his crashed ship and through the wilderness towards the city. Walking for miles in the wilderness, the knight grew tired. Seeing nothing but trees and grass, though he kept walking and walking. He walked until he reached the point where he stood at the gates to the city. The two guards at the gate looked at him, spotting his beaten armor.

"You're not one of the Knights. Where are you from?"

"I'm from the outer rim of this sector. I need to speak with the Knights of the Covenant. It is urgent that I do so."

"Very well."

The armored guards opened the gates and allowed the knight to enter into the city. He walked down the straight street, heading towards the temple. The residents outside the homes looked at the knight. Spotting his armor and they shook their heads with confusion. He continued to walk past them as they did not know who he was or why he is there. The knight arrived at the temple doors and knocked. He knocked continuously until they opened. He looked up and was face to face with one of the Abhdi Knights.

"Who are you?"

"I can explain. Please."

The Knight nodded and allowed him to enter into the temple. When he walked in, the doors shut behind him and he turned, facing the entire Knights of the Covenant. They were lead by Elder Knight Iscar and they were Knight Galeed, Knight Jadau, Knight Leor, Knight Ahio, Knight Beor, Knight Eliah, Knight Festus, Knight Hanan, Knight Mesha, Knight Oded, Knight Rayen, and Knight Yabel.

"Place him in the middle." Elder Knight Iscar said.

The Knights grabbed him and set him in the middle of the room. Elder Knight Iscar measured the knight, noticing his armor and how it was badly damaged. The other Knights watched him for any certain moves or motions he might make. The knight was on his knees, he raised his head up, seeing Iscar in front of him and the Knights surrounding him.

"Who are you, knight?"

"I am Chorazin. I am from the outer rim of this sector."

"Which sector are you from?"

"Sector IV. I'm from the planet Utomia."

"A Utomian. I see. Care to tell me why your armor is heavily damaged and your purpose for coming here?"

"My armor was damaged in a battle."

"Against whom?"

"I was chosen by my guild to travel to the planet of Kuward and find the Fountain of Healing. I arrived on Kuward and through the search I did find the fountain. But, when I approached it, the sky darkened and thunder had begun to roar in the clouds. Suddenly, I found myself face to face with a knight. A knight that I've never seen or heard. I fought against him, but he was too strong. Too powerful. He nearly killed me until I escaped. He damaged my ship and it crash-landed here in your forest."

"This knight you encountered, did he speak of his name?"

"He did. He called himself The Thunder Knight."

Knight Ahio approached Iscar hastily. Iscar raised his hand toward him. Slowing him down as he approached.

"Elder, if I may speak."

"Why should you speak?"

"Because I might have a solution."

"Go and stand at your place, young Knight."

The Knight returned to his place and Iscar looked back at Chorazin, who was tired and beaten down. He kept himself up on the floor from collapsing.

"I know of this Thunder Knight. I've studied such words that spake of him. Yet, this entity is real and is guarding a fountain that is said to possess healing. Yet, we are the ones who do the healing in this universe. Not some fountain."

"Elder Knight." Knight Yabel said.

"What do you want to speak, Knight?"

"This fountain, let me travel to Kuward. Find it and destroy it. So that it will not be in the hands of Those of the Dekar. Whom may already have the knowledge of such a power. If I come across this Thunder Knight, I will slay him. For the Avior is with me."

"You have valid points, Knight Yabel." Iscar said. "Very well, you are to travel to this planet of Kuward. Find the fountain and destroy it. If you do come across The Thunder Knight, put him out of his existence."

Iscar signals the Knights to leave the temple and they do so. Chorazin is taken in to recuperate his strength and health. Meanwhile, Yabel prepares himself to travel to Kuward. He dressed himself in his silver armor with his white and gold tunic atop it. His golden belt held the tunic in place with the armor and he had a white cloak with gold lining. A hood was also attached to the cloak. His long light brown hair flowed thoruhg the wind as he was placing his equipment and his aduroblade within a Helio Sor ship. Behind him approaches Knight Rayen, one of Yabel's closest friends.

"I've been meaning to ask you how's your wife, brother?"

"She is doing well. The birth of our son keeps her happy and strong."

"What did you name the young one?"

"Ohad Grake."

"Ah. A *praising* one he will become."

"That is the hope of the future."

Rayen watched Yabel prepare the ship. His gear and equipment already in place. Yabel looks at the ship and turns to Rayen. Knowing he's about to leave the planet.

"Make sure you do what you will." Rayen said. "Make no mistakes of any kind."

"I will keep your words close to me, brother."

They exchange handshakes and hug one another. Brothers in arms as the Knights would say.

"Tell Iyera and your son that I will be back."

"I will."

Yabel enters the ship and takes off into the sky in mere seconds. Heading out of the atmosphere of Helio, heading to Kuward.

II
FINDING THE FOUNTAIN

Yabel travels through stellar space, outside of Sector 333, he scouts the surrounding areas for the planet of Kuward. Unsure of its appearance, he only knows it appears as a desert planet from a distance in space, until inching closer to see its green landscape and watery rivers. The planet possesses a mirage technique, different than the other planets. Yabel continues to move through space and see a planet in the distance. It appears as a desert planet. Yabel engages the ship to move faster and it does. He comes closer to the planet and it begins to take shape. Warping itself as Yabel moved closer. When he came near its atmosphere, the desert lands vanished and became a land of grass and clear water. Yabel prepared the ship to make landfall on Kuward.

The ship makes its landing on Kuward and Yabel exits. He sees the grass beneath him and the tree that stand above the ground. Yabel shook his head as he walked away from his ship, with his aduroblade on his left side, walking through the grass fields, searching for the Fountain of Healing. Making his rounds through the lands, slicing down bushes and branches in his way with his aduroblade. He continued to walk and couldn't find the fountain.

"Maybe its further out than expected."

Yabel had returned to his ship and flew towards the other side of the planet and made his landing. Once he exited the ship, the grounds were more solid than lush. Yabel noticed it and kept it in his mind that there's something on this side of the planet that's different than the other. He went ahead walking and he looked out, seeing something in the distance. The sound of water was coming from the location and Yabel ran for it. When Yabel reached what he had seen, it was a castle, next to the castle was the Fountain. Covered with grass and a tree. The water of the Fountain came from a spring nearby. On the tree was a ladle. The stones next to the fountain had a message written on them and it said, *"Those who drink from the Fountain shall be healed forevermore."*

"Is that right." Yabel said.

He grabbed the ladle and as he moved it from the tree, drops of water fell and hit the stones. He stepped upon the encrypted stones, at which the sky began to darken and the wind started to blow. The sounds of birds came from the sky, Yabel looked up and seen them flying away from the location of the Fountain. Yabel looked and seen the gates of the castle open and the thunder roared through the clouds. Yabel could see someone approaching him from the castle, he knew who was coming towards him.

"Here he comes."

The Thunder Knight came from the castle. His presence locked onto Yabel and his black horse neighed alongside the thunder. The Thunder Knight came closer and stopped. He started at Yabel, who stared back. The Thunder Knight jumped off his horse and stood by the Fountain. Dressed in a knightly solid black armor and his eyes were a solid white, he reached to his side, revealing an aduroblade of his own. A solid black blade with white streaks of lightning surrounding it. Yabel nodded and pulled out his aduroblade, which was a green blade with a white aura of energy covering it. Yabel held out his aduroblade and The Thunder Knight did the same.

"You believe that you can drink from the water of this

Fountain?"

"I believe that I can destroy this lying wonder you call a healing place. There is only one who heals those who desire it."

"Not to me!" The Thunder Knight said, holding out his aduroblade.

"Your move." Yabel said.

The Thunder Knight lunged out at Yabel with his aduroblade. Yabel countered his attacks with a series of swipes and kicks. The Thunder Knight swung his aduroblade across the air, Yabel ducked his head as the blade came over him. They collided aduroblades before Yabel pushed him off. Yabel looked for an opening and impaled The Thunder Knight in his abdomen. The Thunder Knight stood still and kicked Yabel to the ground before getting atop his horse and running off.

Yabel approached his ship and from the side hovered out a land-veho, which Yabel went atop and rode off, chasing down The Thunder Knight, who was heading back to the castle. The Thunder Knight removed his left hand from his stomach and his hand was wet with his own blood. He was dying. Yabel continued to chase him down and he inched closer. They came to the castle where The Thunder Knight's horse went through the gate and as Yabel came closer, the gate came down. Yabel made it to the inside, but his land-veho was crushed beneath the gate. Yabel raised himself from the ground and looked, The Thunder Knight had vanished. No sound of the horse was heard and Yabel was inside the castle walls. He went to the gate, but they did not open. He used his aduroblade to cut down the gate, but the gate was made of material of which the aduroblade couldn't penetrate.

"Damn it!"

From the castle windows, looked out a handmaiden.

She was dressed in common apparel, a white and blue dress with a white head covering. She looked out at Yabel and was caught by his presence. His features drew her and his strength impressed her. From the door of the room walked in another woman. This woman was dressed in a pink and red dress and her long blonde hair stood out. Her features were beauties and her voice was soft. She seen her handmaiden looking out the window and she went to see.

"What are you gazing at, my handmaiden?"

"A man, your highness."

"What man?"

"She looked out the window and seen Yabel. Continuing to try and open the gate. She was impressed by his strength and was drawn to his features.

"Who is that man?"

"That man, is what you've been asking for."

The woman started at her handmaiden. Waiting for an answer.

"Your new husband."

The woman looked out at Yabel and gave out a small, but hopeful smile.

III
THE LADY OF THE CASTLE

Yabel continued to try and budge his way out of the castle gates, but nothing could work. He yelled in anger slamming his aduroblade against the solid gate, knowing he was now trapped within the castle with no way of escaping. The woman and her handmaiden watched him yell in anger and could feel it.

"He wants to leave." The handmaiden said.

"We should go down to him." The woman said. "Let him know that he's not alone."

The woman left the room as did the handmaiden. They walked down a set a stairs before reaching the bottom floor and when they did, Yabel was standing in the middle of the room, looking around at the castle and its structure. He was thinking to himself, how could he find a way to blow the castle in order for him to exit. Yabel stood in the middle and was preparing to use the strength of the Avior to blow the entire castle apart and as he was preparing, he seen the woman and her handmaiden standing by the doorway of the castle. Their presence ceased him from destroying it.

"Whatever you're about to do, please don't do it." The woman said.

"Who are you?" Yabel asked. "Why are you within these castle walls? And the other woman?"

"She is my handmaiden. Her name is Ila."

"And what is your name?"

"My name is Ashona and I was once the queen of this

land before it was destroyed by a dark magic. My husband, who was king over the lands of Kuward was killed in a battle against dark forces and they cast a curse on the land, thus creating The Thunder Knight that has roamed this planet for years."

"I am truly sorry for your loss. How can I escape these gates?"

"You cannot." The handmaiden said. "Only the Thunder Knight is allowed to exit the gates."

"I followed him here and he disappeared within an instant. Tell me, where is he so that I may finished what we started back at the Fountain."

"You've seen the Fountain?" Ashona said. "Is it still in one piece?"

"As of this moment. Once I get out of here, I am destroying it and leaving this planet. You can come along if you like. I am fond of your beauty, Ashona."

Her face blushed as she let out a small giggle. In the distance, Yabel could hear horse steps approaching. He looked over behind Ashona and her handmaiden to see The Thunder Knight coming towards them. His aduroblade in hand. Yabel yelled for them to move and as they did, Yabel swiped his aduroblade against The Thunder Knight's own. The Thunder Knight jumped off his horse and faced Yabel. They circled each other and Yabel could see the open wound on The Thunder Knight's abdomen.

"I see that you're wounded."

"For the moment I am wounded. Once I kill you, my wound will be healed by the Fountain."

"We shall see of that."

The Thunder Knight ran toward Yabel and they collided with their aduroblades. Yabel swung against The Thunder Knight's power and might. The Thunder Knight shoved Yabel from him and swiped his left arm, cutting through his armor. The Thunder Knight went to kick Yabel, though he missed and Yabel grabbed The Thunder Knight by his helmet and slammed him onto the ground. While on the ground, The Thunder Knight went to move and was kicked by Yabel. Yabel went to impale him, but The Thunder Knight stood up and punched Yabel, knocking him down.

"Your end is here, Knight!" The Thunder Knight said.

He went to decapitate him, but Yabel raised up his aduroblade against The Thunder Knight. Yabel nodded and jumped behind The Thunder Knight, impaling him again. The Thunder Knight had fell to the ground and Yabel finished it off with the slicing off of The Thunder Knight's head. Ashona and Ila approached Yabel, he reached down and picked up the head of the Thunder Knight, seeing that there was a man underneath the armor. A Kuwardian of the ancient past. The Thunder Knight is dead.

"You killed him." Ashona said. "You kill The Thunder Knight."

"I had no other option. It was combat."

Yabel had looked over to the gates and they had not open. He looked down at the body of The Thunder Knight and it came into his being, without The Thunder Knight, he was stuck in the castle with Ashona and Ila. Yabel walked toward Ashona and grabbed her. He was mesmerized by her beauty.

'If I am to be stuck within the walls of this castle, I will marry you. To make sure that you are kept safe."

"You would do that for me?"

"I would and I am."

They kissed each other and were married right afterwards. During the night, they made love to each other, confirming their marriage. The next morning, Yabel awakens, naked in the bed. He gets up and clothes himself. From the bedroom door enters Ashona, carrying The Thunder Knight's armor. It caught Yabel off guard.

"Why are you carrying the armor of The Thunder Knight?"

"Because, I have to tell you something."

"Do tell."

Ashona went and sat down on the bed, next to Yabel. He placed his hand atop hers and she nodded.

"Go ahead and tell me."

"When my husband was killed. The one who conjured the curse on the land, told us that whomever slays The Thunder Knight during their search for the Fountain of Healing, would become the successor to the title."

"You're saying that I must become the new Thunder Knight?"

"Yes. You must don his armor and carry his aduroblade."

Yabel looked outside the window, looking out at the land that he cannot stand on again. He turned to Ashona and glared at the Thunder Knight's armor. Yabel, completely in love with Ashona and he smiled at her.

"I would do anything for you, Ashona."

"I know that now. But, for us to keep our place here, you must don his armor and takes his place. Protect the Fountain of Healing. For it is all that we now have to call our own."

Yabel struggled within himself. The Avior fighting against his own decisions. He walked over to the armor and looked at it. Yabel has found bliss in his love for Ashona and he nodded.

"I must do what I must."

IV
YABEL, THE KNIGHT OF THUNDER

Within the Temple of the Avior, the Knights have waited days for Yabel to make his return from Kuward, to hear the answer concerning the Fountain of Healing. Yet now, Yabel has not returned to Helio and The Knights are concerned. Elder Knight Iscar commands all of the Knights to present themselves within the main room of the temple to discuss plans of searching for Yabel. Each of the Knights make their way into the main room with Iscar already awaiting them inside.

"Knights of the Abhdi, you know why I've called you up at this moment, one of our Knights, Knight Yabel, has not made his return from Kuward. Which means something has taken place. As of this moment, I will send you all to Kuward to find Knight Yabel and bring him back here. Whether he be alive or dead, find him."

The Knights nodded to Iscar and immediately gathered themselves toward a series of three Helio Sor ships. Between the three ships, Knight Rayen, Knight Galeed, Knight Jadeu, and Knight Leor were set in one. Knight Ahio, Knight Beor, Knight Eliah, and Knight Festus were set within the second one. The third ship was compiled of Knight Hanan, Knight Mesha, and Knight Oded. The ships each took off on their set time and flew up into the Helio sky and left the atmosphere. The ships trailed each other, setting their courses on Kuward.

Taking a shortcut with stellarspeed, the Helio Sor ships bursts themselves through the skies of Kuward and make a landing nearby the open field. As the ships settle, the Knights exit from them. On the side of the field, the Knights noticed another Helio Sor. Sitting as if it has been there for some time. The Knights knew this is where Yabel had made landfall. All dressed in their silver-clad armor and tunics of various colors pertaining to the Avior. They each grabbed their aduroblades from the ships and proceeded to walk through the field, searching for Yabel. While making their steps, they notice footsteps on the grounds. They match similar to the boots of an Abhdi Knight. The Knights knew these footsteps belonged to Yabel and moved with a quicker pace, following the footsteps.

"He must be close by!" Knight Ahio yelled.

"Keep your eyes open, Knights." Knight Rayen said. "For we do not know what lurks through these lands."

They continued their walking only to hear the sound of water flowing. They kept moving and finally came upon the Fountain of Healing, sitting in front of them and the castle within the distance. The Knights moved steady. Seeing the Fountain in front of them and it was not damaged. Not a scratch or mark on it.

"Keep your blades steady." Rayen declared.

They took slow steps toward the Fountain. They inched closer and closer by each footstep. Once they came upon the Fountain, Rayen looked down at the stones and noticed the markings of writing on them. He measured it with his eyes, the other Knights were not sure of what to make of it.

"What is inscribed on the stones?" Knight Galeed asked Rayen.

"Those who drink from the Fountain shall be healed forevermore."

Rayen took a step atop the stones and the wind had begun to blow, the sky had darkened above them. Birds flew over them, gawking at the sounds of the thunder roaring from above them in the clouds. The Knights gathered themselves in a circle, keeping their eyes on their surroundings. They each pulled out their aduroblades. The light of the blades increased their sight from the dark sky.

In the distance, they could hear the sounds of a horse galloping. The sound was growing and increasing. They looked and seen the figure coming toward them. It was The Thunder Knight, atop his black horse and his aduroblade on his side. The Knights made a line and stood in front of The Thunder Knight with the Fountain in between them. His horse stopped as he started at the eleven Knights.

"You believe you can drink from the water of this Fountain?" The Thunder Knight explained.

"No." Rayen said. "We believe we can destroy this Fountain and find our brother, who happen to arrive here not too long ago."

"I know not of your brother. All that I know is to keep this Fountain protected throughout all of its days."

The Thunder Knight jumped from his horse and stood before the Knights. He reached over to his side and pulled out his aduroblade from its sheath. The solid black blade with its white streaks of lightning made some of the Knights uncomfortable and unaware of such a blade. Rayen stood boldly in front of The Thunder Knight.

"If you want a challenge, you will have one with me."

The Thunder Knight raised his hand up to Rayen. Pausing him. The Thunder Knight shook his head in shame as he gazed at the other Knights. He pointed his aduroblade toward them. Each one of them.

"I can see you're their leader. Let your brethren face

me first. If they do not succeed, you will have the honor of facing me yourself. A fair challenge wouldn't you say."

Rayen took a step back, placing his aduroblade back into its sheath. He allowed each of the Knights to combat The Thunder Knight. Knight Galeed was first. He stood in front of The Thunder Knight with his aduroblade, which was coated in a blue energy and the blade glowed brightly. The two engaged in combat with The Thunder Knight injuring him with a swipe to his left arm. Knight Jadau was second to combat The Thunder Knight. Jadeu stood tall with his yellow-energy coated aduroblade and fought against The Thunder Knight.

Knight Jadeu didn't succeed as his right leg was sliced by The Thunder Knight. Jadeu sat on the ground, next to Galeed. Rayen stood by them, watching The Thunder Knight's moves in combat. The Thunder Knight asked again for the next challenger and Knight Leor was that challenge. With his blue-bladed and white-coated aduroblade, he went against The Thunder Knight. Clashing their blades together before he was elbowed in the face by The Thunder Knight. Knight Ahio went against The Thunder Knight with his glowing light green aduroblade. After Ahio had lost, Knight Beor went against him. Swinging and slashing his dark yellow aduroblade against The Thunder Knight, the Thunder Knight kicked Beor and slammed him onto the dry ground.

"Where is a real challenge?!" The Thunder Knight shouted. "Keep them coming until I face one!"

Knight Eliah was next and took his twirling abilities of his white-bladed and gold-coated aduroblade against The Thunder Knight,. Almost on par with his strikes and swipes, The Thunder Knight emitted a small array of lightning from his blade against Eliah, tossing him onto the ground. Knight Festus and Knight Hanan were no successful in their bouts against The Thunder Knight. Festus used his orange-coated adurtoblade against him and failed. As did Hanan with his dark orange-coated aduroblade.

"There's something about him, Rayen." Knight Eliah said. "Something that seems quite familiar."

"I have noticed it."

Knight Mesha went against The Thunder Knight. Using his white-bladed and light blue-coated aduroblade. Mesha was fast in combat, but his speed was unable to give him the victory against The Thunder Knight. To which The Thunder Knight had caught onto his quick moves and stopped him before he could continue further. Knight Oded went against The Thunder Knight with a rough and rugged attacks. Swiging and clasing against The Thunder Knight with his dark green aduroblade, Oded used his strength against The protector of the Fountain, though, The Thunder Knight was also strong in strength and used it against Oded. Defeating him after slamming him against the Fountain itself. Rayen looked at the Knights, all were defeated. The thunder Knight turned his gaze onto Rayen, pointing at him with his aduroblade.

"Your turn, leader of these Knights! Prove to me that you are able to match my feats!"

"I will prove to you much more than that."

Rayen removed his cloak and stood in front of The Thunder Knight. He reached over and raised up his aduroblade, the white-blade and its gold-aura glared against The Thunder Knight's black and white aduroblade. They clashed the blades in combat. Using twirls, swipes, and slashes against one another. Both are on par with each other. Neither of the two are able to surpass the other and their skills are almost identical. The other Knights take note of the fight and watch as Rayen and The Thunder Knight battle. Both use their speed and their strength against the other, but it appears the same for them both. They pause for a brief moment, remobilizing their similar skill sets.

"You fight like someone I know." Rayen said.

"You do not know me, Knight. I am beyond your comprehension."

The Thunder Knight went to impale Rayen, though he moved over and caught The Thunder Knight's aduroblade against his own. Rayen punched the Knight in the face and elbowed him backwards. Rayen took his aduroblade and swiped it against his chest and handed him an uppercut with his right fist. The Thunder Knight stumbled back with his feet as his helmet had flew up into the air and fell into the Fountain. He raised his head up as his light-brown hair was flowing. Rayen looked at him and knew who he was seeing.

"Yabel?" Rayen responded.

The other Knights looked in what appeared to be shock. Staring at Yabel, dressed up as The Thunder Knight. Rayen approached him and shook him. Trying to get Yabel to his senses.

"Yabel! It is us!" Rayen shouted. "Yabel, it's me, Rayen of Grake!"

Yabel slowly looked at Rayen. He looked closer into his eyes and let out a smile. His grabbed Rayen and hugged him tightly.

"Rayen!" Yabel stammered. "I didn't know it was you I was fighting against."

"Neither did we know it was you."

Yabel looked at the other Knights, all of whom holding their wounds as they look at him with confusion and forgiveness. Yabel stood in front of them and apologized to them all. Rayen looked outward toward the castle.

"What happened to you out here?"

"I landed here and came to the Fountain. I fought The Thunder Knight, chased him into that castle and killed him there. Then, I became The Thunder Knight. Now, you've set me free."

"Great to hear that."

Rayen looked at the armor Yabel was wearing and could tell that it wasn't his ordinary Abhdi uniform nor was the aduroblade he was carrying. He took another look back at the castle before putting his focus on Yabel.

"Where is your uniform and aduroblade, brother?"

"Within the walls of the castle. Without the existence of The Thunder Knight, no one can enter or leave the castle."

"Well, you are dressed up as him and you carry his blade. Go an get your belongs. We're leaving this planet and heading home."

"I will do so." Yabel said.

He rode off atop the black horse and reentered the castle. Within the walls, Ashona and her handmaiden were asleep. Yabel grabbed his uniform and aduroblade. He left the castle before kissing Ashona on her cheek.

"I will not forget you, my love."

Yabel returned to the Knights and with their aduroblades together, using the Avior as a source for its power, they destroyed the Fountain and blew it apart. They each entered their Helio Sor ships and flew off Kuward, returning to Helio.

V
THE OLD WAYS OF BEFORE

Making their way back to Helio, after the exit the atmosphere of Kuward, the memories of Ashona were wiped away from Yabel's mind. As if he never met her to begin with. Flying through the depths of outer space, the Knights recuperate within the ships. Rayen sat next to Yabel, checking up on him. Seeing him trying to get his mind on track after what had just happened on Kuward.

"Are you going to be alright?" Rayen asked.

"I will be fine." Yabel said. "I just need some rest time and I will be back like myself."

Rayen nodded and walked away from Yabel, as he sat in his seat with his eyes closed. Trying to fall asleep. Back on Kuward, Ashona awakens from her sleep to find Yabel gone from the castle. She sent Ila to go and search the castle for Yabel. Ila went ahead and searched the entire castle. From top to bottom. She returned to Ashona's chambers and told her of Yabel's disappearance. Ashona cried loudly and set herself apart from the castle within her chambers. As she cried, Ila walked away from the chamber doors, to give Ashona some space to herself. Though within the chambers, Ashona crouched down and reached for something beneath her bed. She pulls out a chest, a medium sized stone-like carved chest.

She opened the chest and from it appeared a shadow being, somewhat of a spiritual nature. The shadow almost looked dwarfish in a way. Though a solid black figure it was.

"I have a message I need you to send for me." Ashona

told the shadow.

"What is this message." The Shadow replied. "I am eager to know of it before I sent it over."

"There was a man here. His name is Yabel. I need you to go out and find him. Tell him that he needs me and I need him."

"Madam, the universe is a vast place. Filled with many lands and obstacles, how will I know how to find this Yabel you have spoken of?"

"You will know of him. He possessed an aura of immense power. Something that I've never felt before. That is what made him different than the rest who have been here. Now, find him and tell him what I have said to you."

"As you command, madam." The shadow said, vanishing away from the chamber and making its way through the vast sight of the stellar space.

The Knights returned to Hleio and enter the gates of Tropoloton with their residents cheering for their return as of Yabel's comeback. The Knights enter the temple as Iscar approaches them. Greeting each of them. Iscar turned and seen Yabel standing in the midst of them. He approached him joyously and hugged Yabel.

"I had begun to wonder where you have gone."

"I understand, Elder Knight." Yabel said. "It was a strange one for me as well."

"I know you'll need some time to yourself. Go on."

"Yes, my Master."

Yabel left the temple rooms and returned to his chambers. Within his chambers, he sat atop his bed, trying to wonder what was on his mind. As if something was pricking his brain for answers pertaining to Kuward. Within the silent and chilly room, the shadow messenger appeared before Yabel within a second. The messenger caught Yabel off guard as he grabbed quickly for his audroblade, ready to strike down the messenger.

"Wait a second, Knight of the Abhdi." The Messenger said. "I come with a purposeful intent."

"How so?" Yabel asked, holding his aduroblade tightly.

"You might be wondering why your head is aching."

"How do you know that?"

"Because I have the answers you are seeking from within your memory."

"Do tell me of these memories that I have seemed to forget. For my spirit calls for it."

"The reason why your mind is in the pain that is inflicting you is because of your lost memories of a woman."

"What do you mean a woman? What woman?"

"Back when you were on Kuward, you met a woman. A beautiful woman. Now, she has sent me to tell you that she needs you and you need her."

"Preposterous! How am I supposed to believe the words from a shadow messenger? One that appears without a true form?"

"I have a true form, but it would crumble your entire city and your temple along with it."

"I still do not believe the words you have spoken."

"Don't worry about my words, Knight of the Abhdi. Concern yourself with your thoughts, for they will reveal themselves this very night and then, you will remember the memories of old. The old ways of before."

The Messenger disappeared from Yabel's sight. He calmed himself down and placed his aduroblade into its sheath and laid down atop his bed. Within his sleep, he dreamt of Ashona and she called out to him. He could recognize her and all the memories he had of his time on Kuward were returning to him through his sleep. Once the last memory returned to him, Yabel jumped up from his bed. No more is he tired and wanting to sleep. He's full of energy and knows all that happened on Kuward. When the morning had struck, Yabel came down to the temple to meet with Iscar, whom was standing inside the temple. Iscar and Yabel went into one of the temple rooms to speak.

"What is it, Yabel?" Iscar asked. "I can sense something within your being. You're full of energy. No longer are you tired and weak. Something has happened to you."

"My Master, back when I was on Kuward. During the days when I did not make my return, I met a woman there and I married her."

"You did?"

"I couldn't remember anything that happened on Kuward until last night. A messenger came to me and told me of the things that happened on Kuward."

"What kind of messenger spoke to you, Knight?"

"A shrouded one. He was covered from head to toe in shadow. His height was about the height of a dwarf. Though, I could sense that he wasn't from Sudravor. I know not of his whereabouts."

"But, this messenger came to you during the night and told you of this woman you've married back on Kuward?"

"He did and the memories returned to me during my slumber. I remember everything that happened on Kuward. From my landing drop to fighting The Thunder Knight to marrying her. I remember it all now."

"Tell me, what is this woman's name?"

"Ashona is her name. I had saved both her and her handmaiden from The Thunder Knight before I slayed him within the castle walls."

"So, what is it you ask of me this day?"

"I ask of you to allow me to return to Kuward, bring

Ashona and her handmaiden back here. To live with me."

Iscar nodded. He fully understood Yabel's intentions on retrieving Ashona from Kuward. Though, he could sense something else within Yabel. Something was tearing at him from the inside. The very inside.

"I will allow you to go out there and bring her and her handmaiden back."

"Thank you, my Master."

"But I will warn you, Knight Yabel. Your spirit, its tearing slowly, but the tear is strong. You're being pulled in a tug of war between the Avior and the Dekar. The Avior is trying to give you happiness and contentment. The Dekar is trying to seduce you with your anger and self-will. Truly, all of your choices and decisions are in your hands, Knight. Use them properly and keep yourself at watch."

"I will do as you have said, Master." Yabel replied.

He left the temple and prepared one of the Helio Sor ships and set his map for Kuward. The ship hovered itself and boasted into the sky, where all of the Knights and the residents were able to witness it. The residents wondered why is he leaving once again and the Knights had wondered will they have to face him again in combat, believing that this time they may fall to his blade.

VI
A LOVER'S TRAIL

Flying through outer space, Yabel keeps his eyes on the map, navigating his way toward Kuward. He knows that he must keep himself on guard. For he now feels the tugging within his being. The Avior against The Dekar, the ancient war taking place within his body as he fought within it on the outside. Yabel placed the ship into hyperspace and vanished out of Sector 333.

The ship exits stellar speed, now entering into the atmosphere of Kuward. As the ship landed, Yabel remembers the locations of the land and quickly makes his movement toward the castle. As he ran, he passed by the decimated ruins of the Fountain of Healing. Its water had dried out and the tree and grass around it were dying. The ladle was also destroyed along with the Fountain. Yabel approached the castle, seeing its gates were opened. Yabel ran through the castle, yelling for Ashona and Ila. He could not find them. On his way out of the castle, he seemed to have found a note left behind. Yabel picked up the note and read it. The note had spoken of Ashona, being taken captive by the Viper Order and placed on numerous planets throughout the universe. The Viper Lords know about Yabel and Ashona marriage and are using it to their advantage.

Yabel, now angry with both himself and the Viper Order, leaves the castle and enters back into his ship. Flying off from Kuward. Yabel now makes it his mission to travel throughout the universe to find Ashona and Ila. Even if it means losing himself in the process of finding them, he will see to it that she and Ila are both kept safe by the Knights of the Covenant.

"I will find you both." Yabel said to himself. "I will find you both."

Yabel flew through outer space and he gazed the planets that were around the area within the sector. Monitoring them on the map within the ship. He looked over to his left to another planet. Which was lush with grass and trees. Almost the entire planet was a forest planet. Its named was Darella and it was Yabel's first place to approach in searching for Ashona. The Helio Sor ship went ahead and dove down into the atmosphere of Darella. Getting ready to make landfall within the jungles of the planet.

VII
THE GIANTS OF DARELLA

Yabel exited the ship and looked around at his surroundings. Only seeing trees, tall trees. Covered in green leaves and grass which stood almost three feet in height. Yabel could also see mountains in the horizon. He went ahead and walked through the grass to find clues that would refer to Ashona's whereabouts. Through the tall grass and tall trees, Yabel couldn't see anything in his paths. He could only green, dark green, and the brownish bark of the tall trees. Yabel's aduroblade swiped a clear path through the grass and trees for him to continue further along and once he stood out in an open space. A small field to where he could see the land around him in the distance. Sitting before him was a large mountain. Brown and gray and rugged. Yabel looked closely and could see openings within the walls of the mountain.

"Maybe she is in there." Yabel said. "I will have to search it."

Yabel walked toward the mountain and its height grew by each of Yabel's steps. He began to wonder what the wildlife of Darella could be. Passing by skeletal remains of different animal species. From birds to mammals to reptiles to insects. He continued to walk, and he found his foot within a footprint. Very large and his foot was only within the middle of the footprint. The print mesmerizing Yabel. Nodding at the size of the print within the grass and dirt. He measured the print, studying it with the knowledge that he possessed and the ground shook. Three times the ground had shaken and

Yabel hid himself beside a boulder that sat on the bottom edge of the mountain. The shaken continued to grow and it was coming from within the mountain.

Yabel peeked to look and he seen three giants exiting the mountain. All three of them were hairy from the head down and they wore loincloth made out of animal skin and flesh. Their height stood up to ten to fifteen feet tall and their stench was of decay and sweat. Yabel watched them stand by the mountain, speaking to one another in their language, presumably a form of Darellian speech. Yabel went to move himself from the boulder to the trees and the trees shook, getting the giants' attention. They turned and growled at the trees, believing to frighten off an animal. Though, they didn't stop there and they each grabbed their battle clubs from the mountain's entrance and begun to swipe down the trees in front of them to catch a kill.

"This isn't going as planned." Yabel said, moving around beneath the fallen trees.

The giants continued until one of them spotted Yabel moving beneath the debris. The giant roared and pointed at the spot, to where the other giants ran over, kicking the debris and Yabel into the air. The giants seen Yabel, standing on his feet facing them. The giants roared at him, holding their clubs up high. Yabel, removing leaves from his hair, smirked, reaching for his aduroblade.

"I wasn't expecting to face giants this day. But, looks like I may have no other option."

Yabel raised up his aduroblade and pointed it toward the giants. The giants didn't know what to make of the weapon. For they've never seen a weapon that glowed with such energy and power. The aduroblade intrigued them and they desired to have it. The three giants ran toward Yabel as did he. The giants raised up their clubs, slamming them into the ground. Yabel ducking his head and rolling out of their sight to avoid the falling clubs. Yabel swiped the aduroblade against their ankles and feet, slowing them down for a moment. Yabel continued to fight against them from the ground. He jumped up onto one of the giants' sides, climbing upon him and impaling him in his arms and chest with the aduroblade. The giant roared in pain as it grabbed Yabel, towing him into the mountain.

"Almost finished with them." Yabel said. "I know I can get past them."

The wind had started to pick up, getting Yabel and the giants' attention. From the sky came down large birds with massive wingspans. They appeared to have the features of both eagles and vulture. Their features were as white as snow and their beaks were as gold as the Tropolton streets.

These creatures are called the Nphippors. The pipers came down and grabbed each of the giants with their talons, brought them up into the air and tossed them across the fields of Darella, away from the mountain. Yabel looked up at the giant birds and nodded. The nphippors screeched and flew away. Yabel turned to the mountain and entered it. Within the mountain was the lair of the giants. Flesh, weapons, and cloths from previous visitors of the planet were within the mountain's walls. Though, Yabel caught something of interest. There was a map carved into the stone walls of the mountain. Yabel recognized the locations presented onto the map. He seen Darella and there was a trail, leading back to Kuward, though it presented a trail. One that left Darella and came to a planet called Ivil. The planet of three days of darkness and three days of light. Yabel could sense that is the location where Ashona has been moved to.

"I am coming for you, Ashona. I promise I am coming."

Yabel returned to his Helio Sor ship and left the planet of Darella. Making his way toward the planet of Ivil.

95

VIII
THREE NIGHTS AND THREE DAYS

Yabel makes his way toward the planet of Ivil which resides in the sector of Star 895. Yabel looked ahead towards the planet, seeing its dark nature mixed with its light nature. The planet had one red sun and a white moon. Yabel also noticed its desert lands on one side and a grassy plain on the other. The ship had entered into Ivil's atmosphere and had begun to land within the desert lands. Once the ship made its landing, Yabel exited and started to walk around the desert lands in search for Ashona.

Continuing his walk, several miles out, away from his ship, Yabel could hear rustling through the sand and sounds of pacing coming from around his location. Yabel continued to walk, steady and slowly, listening to the sounds that were coming from around him. His right hand laid onto his aduroblade's handle. Yabel took another step and standing in front of him were three Kanotes, dog-like creatures that possessed enhanced strength and speed. Their eyes were gold and their fur was a mixture of gold, black, and red. Their ears stood tall as did their four legs. Their snouts were long as an average dog, though their teeth were sharp and rigid. The kanotes started barking at Yabel, who stayed still, hoping the kanotes do not attack him. He keeps taking his steps, but the kanotes followed him. Growling at him and snarling. Their mouths had begun to foam and Yabel knew what he had to do.

The kanotes barked and ran toward Yabel, lunging

themselves into the air at him. Yabel could hear them and he pulled out his aduroblade and sliced the first kanote in half. Its body fell into the golden sand and the other kanotes looked at Yabel and the dead kanote. They nodded and ran after Yabel, clamping their jaws onto his armored arms and legs. Yabel struggled to fight off the two remaining kanotes. The aduroblade swiped across and decapitated the kanote that clamped against his right leg. Yabel tossed the last kanote off his left arm and they had a stare down. The last kanote barked at Yabel, who twirled his aduroblade and pointed it toward the kanote.

"Your move." Yabel said.

The kanote ran toward Yabel and he twisted the aduroblade against the running kanote, creating a force of energy which he pushed against the kanote, knocking it far away from their location. Not knowing if the creature had died or survived. Yabel looked around, not seeing any more kanotes.

"The beasts of the field." He said to himself before continuing on further.

Moving along further, Yabel had begun to notice the sun was going down and the moon was rising up. He later found a rocky cave within the desert and decided to search it. He entered the cave and walked through it, only finding remains of other kanotes and creatures that roam the desert lands of Ivil. As Yabel was searching, he noticed something different about the planet's structure. He begun o realize that the moon was sitting in place of the sun and that hours had already passed by, but the sun didn't rise. Still searching the desert lands in the dark, a day had passed. The second day was covered in darkness and so was the third day. Throughout those days did Yabel go out through the desert lands of Ivil to search for Ashona, using his aduroblade as a source of light to see through the thick darkness. He proved unsuccessful in his searching.

Yabel kept walking and searching. As he found himself stepping on sand covered grass, he looked out and seen the grassy plain of the planet and above him, the sun was rising and the moon was setting. He walked through the grassy plain, seeing life of animals and insects roaming through the fields. The grassy plains were filled with life and peace as the desert lands were filled with death and torment. He found a set of trees standing before him and carved into the trees was a message. Yabel had put the message together with the knowledge that he had and spoke it out of his mouth.

"Your wife, Ashona, belongs to Skotos. The planet of The Dark Lord of the Shaman. If you seek her life, come to Skotos and claim her as your own or leave her be with the Skotos Lord."

Yabel prepared himself and returned to his ship after another long walk. Returning to his ship, he entered and left the planet of Ivil, heading for the planet of Skotos, which resided in Sector V of the universe.

IX
THE DARK LORD

Traveling to Sector V, where Skotos is located, Yabel prepares himself for the fight he will have to endure to get Ashona and Ila off the planet and from The Dark Lord of the Shaman. Traveling through the sector, Yabel looked at the planets of the sector. He could see Ordow, the planet of the Magus Court, Dagobar, the planet of the Orchs and Trolls, Darella, the planet that he previously visited with the giants, Zappdow, a planet with constant thunderstorms, Kingod, the planet consumed with elemental technology, Thran, the war planet, and Skotos, the clouded planet of The Dark Lord of the Shaman. Heading to Skotos, Yabel noticed the clouds covering the planet were only a trick and he entered into its atmosphere, seeing nothing but the planet's dark blue and dark violet sky. Its clouds were black, and thunder roared over the air.

"She must be in there." Yabel said, looking out toward a dark castle.

Yabel landed the ship in front of the castle, seeing it was in the middle of a city, a deserted city filled with silence, as if the city was once occupied. Yabel exited the ship and approached the dark castle. Its gates had risen up from the ground to give him entrance. Yabel entered the castle, somewhat reminiscent of the castle back on Kuward. But, there was a darkness covering this castle. An ancient darkness. Within the walls of the castle, Yabel could sense a dark presence watching over him. Yabel walked up the staircase, heading up to the top of the castle.

"You can show yourself, Dark Lord." Yabel said. "I'm here."

From the door of the castle opened and out came The Dark Lord of the Shaman. A tall, intimidating figure of a man. Whose hair was black as the clouds and was down to his upper arms. His face was thin and had a goatee. He wore leather and armored clothing with a black cloak. He also wore fingerless gloves and on his side was blade of his own, a Skotosian blade.

"You have made yourself seen, Knight of the Covenant."

"I know you have Ashona and Ila here and I want them set free from your hand."

"I have no issue setting them free. That is, if you can master me in combat."

"You challenge me to a battle in order to give them freedom?"

"That is what I have spoken, is it not. Face me, defeat me, and they will be set free from my hand and into yours."

Yabel nodded and pulled out his aduroblade. The Dark Lord laughed at Yabel, raising up his Skotosian blade, which was black and covered with a dark violet aura of energy. It gave off a chilling hum.

"Are you ready, Knight?"

"I am prepared."

"Good."

Yabel and The Dark Lord engage into combat. Slamming their blades and clashing them against one another. Yabel swiped across the air as did The Dark Lord, though he used an invisible energy to grab Yabel and toss him against the wall. Taking Yabel by surprise.

"What was that?"

"Skotosian magic. Something you did not sense when you entered into its atmosphere. You have a blindness in you."

"That will not stop me from defeating you, Shaman of Skotos."

"We will see."

They continued in their combat. Their blades clash, shaking the castle walls through their power. The Dark Lord swiped the aduroblade out of Yabel's hand and hits him in the head with his Skotosian blade. Yabel fell to the cold ground, reaching for his aduroblade that lies within his sight. The Dark Lord scoffed at Yabel, laughing at him on the ground.

"It appears that I have defeated a Knight of the Covenant. I thought you Knights were beyond powerful. That you possessed a power that many within the universe fear. I've heard your power matches the Dekar and is even stronger than it. How come I do not sense that power coming from you? Are you really a Knight or are you just a mere scoundrel?"

Yabel continued to reach for the aduroblade and his eyes began to glow a golden color. The aduroblade started to shake and Yabel's eyes were gold as of a golden flame and the aduroblade started to twirl out of control.

"What are you doing?" The Dark Lord said.

"I am in your hands now." Yabel said in the open. "Enter me once more and aid me. I ask of it as humbly as I can. Aid me."

The aduroblade stopped twirling and swooped across the ground and back into Yabel's hand. His eyes were still gold. Yabel stood up, facing The Dark Lord, who could see a change in Yabel and seen his eyes were gold. The Dark Lord could feel an energy surrounding Yabel, a power he has not known.

"I am still standing, Shaman of Skotos."

"As am I."

The Dark Lord ran toward Yabel with his blade and Yabel raised his hand up, stopping The Dark Lord in his steps. Struggling to release himself from the hold.

"What is this you have bounded onto me?!"

"The Avior has a hold on you." Yabel said. "Allow me to give you the release."

Yabel raised up his aduroblade and slashed the chest of The Dark Lord and with the power of the Avior, tossed him outside of the castle walls and he fell to the ground. Yabel defeated The Dark Lord and the Avior guided him to another part of the castle, where Ashona and Ila were kept prisoner. Yabel entered the dungeon of the castle, seeing them behind the cell doors.

"Yabel?!" Ashona let out.

"Is it him?!" Ila asked.

"It is me." Yabel replied. "I'm getting you two out of here."

Yabel raised up his aduroblade and cut the lock off the door. He opened it, releasing them and they ran out to hug him. He hugged them back and they left the dungeon and the castle, making their way toward the ship. While running out of the castle, Yabel looked over and seen a small puddle of blood, where The Dark Lord had fell. Though, his body was nowhere to be seen. Yabel nodded as they entered the ship and took off, leaving the planet of Skotos and returning to Helio.

X
SALVATION TO COME

Yabel makes his return to Helio, but notices something strange taking place with the city of Tropolton. Ashona and Ila look out of the window toward the city and they see what Yabel is seeing. The Viper Lords have invaded the lands and their army of Rainshockers are roaming through the streets of the city. They can see the residents in harm and the Knights fighting against the rainshockers in front of the temple. Yabel cannot stand to watch and he lands the ship on the outside of the city. They exit the ship, hearing the sounds of screams and blasts.

"I am going to take you someplace safe." Yabel said.

"What about you, beloved?" Ashona asked. "Where will you go?"

"I will fight alongside my brothers. I am a Knight after all."

"Go." Ila said. "Lead us to the safe place and aid your brothers in arms."

Yabel nodded as they slowly entered the city. He tells Ashona and Ila to remain with the building that sits near the gates of the city, for many outsiders do not seek to approach it, believing it to be a useless building. While they waited inside, Yabel rain through the streets with his aduroblade, swiping and killing the rainshockers that were around him. His blade cutting through their armor. The residents looked out and seen Yabel.

"Yabel has returned to us!" The residents cheered.

"Go someplace safe and we will wipe this city of its invaders!"

The residents returned to their homes while Yabel fought off the rain shockers that were in his way. He looked out in front, seeing the Knights battling against rainshockers and the two Viper Lords, Sinth Julius and Sinth Juliana. They carried and fought against the Knights with their aduroblades and Sinthblade. Rainshockers continued to fire their plasma-ranges at Yabel, who reflected their blasts back to them.

"Brothers!" Yabel yelled.

The Knights looked and seen Yabel running toward them. They filled up with joy seeing their fellow brother return.

"Something's taking place." Sinth Julius said. "I don't like it!"

Sinth Julius could feel the power of the Avior rising up within the city, bringing him to fear. He grabbed Juliana by her arm, rallied the remaining rain shockers to return to their ships as did he run back to his ship. Once Yabel reached the Knights and the temple, the Viper Lords had already hovered into the air and flew away with the rainshockers with them.

"Next time." Yabel said, watching them leave the planet.

The Knights celebrate their victory against the Viper Order and the return of Yabel. They rejoice and Yabel introduces Ashona and Ila to them. They greet them as if they were of their own family. Elder Knight Iscar meets Ashona and Ila. He greets them and looked at Ashona closely. She doesn't know what's going on and neither does Yabel. Iscar looks at Yabel. Iscar was searching her spirit and caught something else within her.

"It appears that she is with child, Knight Yabel. Your child."

Ashona turned to Yabel, unable to speak a word. Yabel looked at her and smiled. Iscar nodded.

"She is truly your wife indeed."

Yabel and Ashona hugged one another with smiles on their faces.

Many months later, Yabel had also taken Ila to be a wife of his own and Ashona gives birth to a son. Yabel and Ashona discuss a name for their son and Yabel has chosen a name.

"What do you want to name him?" Ashona said.

"Sephor."

"I've never heard of it before. Where does it come from?"

"A family lineage from father to son. Sephor Serkelrod is his name.

YABEL
AND THE LOST GRAIL
A MYSTICAL HUNT OF THE *EVER WAR* UNIVERSE

690 BOC
690 YEARS DURING THE *BATTLE OF CAELUM*

I
LOST IN HISTORY

The Knights of the Covenant collide with the Sinstorians on the planet of Thran. The Sinstorians have challenged the Knights to a battle in order to determine who will overtake the planet of Helio. The Knights are aware of these coming battles since the War of Helio began. Fighting his way through the battlefield is Knight Yabel Serkelrod. Now a Knight Commander, rallies the other Knights to walk along with him into battle. Standing by his side is Knight Rayen Grake, also has become a Knight Commander. The Knights on the field follow the two Commanders into battle against the Sinstorians.

"For The High One!" Yabel yelled.

The Knights yelled with their might, running towards the Sinstorians. Who race toward the Knights on their chariots and horses. Dressed in their golden armor and carrying with them their swords and spears. Few wielded bows and arrows. Leading the Sinstorians is Amten, one of the great Governors of Sinstor. Wearing his Yeor armor covered with scales and a hard hide, his countenance is harsh and he is determine to destroy the Knights on the battlefield. Leaving their bodies to rot with the fuming heat of Thran.

"We must eliminate them all!" Amten yelled. "Once that is done, we will have their planet!"

Both sides determine to win the battle and eventually the war itself. Fighting for ages, the two sides collide. The Sinstorians' swords clash with the Knights' aduroblades. Most of the Sinstorian soldiers only carried swords, whereas Amten possessed an aduroblade of his own. A golden blade detained with blue lining and with a bright white glow. The hilt was made of gold and engraved on the hilt was an image and the name of Sinstor's Pharao Sebek-Em-Of. Fighting off the Knights in an equal bout. Through the battle, Yabel noticed Amten's aduroblade.

"I will take their leader, Rayen." Yabel said.

"Are you sure of it?"

"I am. I'll finish the job."

Rayen nodded and Yabel ran for Amten. Yabel swiped the aduroblade against any Sinstorian soldier that came into his way. Amten could spot Yabel coming for him and it excited him. Amten smiled as he stood out in the open. His arms stretched out.

"Come and face me, Knight! I will show you who's god rules the universe!"

Yabel stood in front of Amten. Measuring his stance and recognizing his Yeor armor. The armor impressed Yabel, never to have seen anything like it before in battle.

"You wear the hide of a Yeor Dragon."

"I know you aren't aware of the customs to Sinstorians. We are more powerful than anyone in all the sectors. You only have one god to talk to. We have many."

"Yes, I know. I figured we'll fight today and see who's god is with who."

"I was hoping you'll say that." Amten said, raising up his aduroblade.

Yabel raised up his own and the two stood across from one another. Yabel's face showed focus and Amten's only showed a smile. Growing as the seconds pass. Amten clashed his blade against Yabel's. They clashed once more with sparks flying from the impact and the low-pitched sound of thunder following. The remaining Knights and Sinstorians soldiers continue to battle. They clashed again, this time with Yabel getting the upper hand. He elbows Amten in the face and trips him with his leg. Amten fell to the ground and flips himself up onto his feet.

"I am not like those you have encountered before." Amten said. "I am a Governor of Sinstor. I possess great power."

"Why don't you use it."

Yabel swings his aduroblade, crashing it into the Yeor armor. The armor is too dense to cut through. Impressing Yabel. Amten lunges toward Yabel with his blade, twirling the blade and slamming it consecutive times. Yabel kept his balance as he blocks the attacks from Amten.

"You have nothing else to give?" Amten asked.

"I might have something in mind."

From Yabel's left hand arose a flame. This flame wasn't the same glow as an ordinary flame. The flame from Yabel's hand was green and Yabel's pupils turned green as the flame increased. Yabel raised his left hand, grabbing the air, in which he pulled it down and pressed it toward Amten, releasing a blast of energy emitted from the green flame. Amten is shoed across the field, rolling on the ground. He regains his stance as his armor begins to crack.

"What was that power?" Amten said.

Yabel approached him, walking. He could see the crack in the armor. He now had his opportunity to strike.

"What power was that?" Amten asked. "I want to know!"

"That power comes from The High One. It's called the

Avior."

"I've never heard of such power. Nor have I ever seen it."

"Because you're not one of His. Even if you manage to comprehend this power, your obsession with your Sinstorian gods would've blinded you to the power."

"No matter." Amten said, standing on his feet. "The Mystical Ones will grant me a power far stronger than your god could ever conjure."

"Then, where are your gods, Governor?"

Amten paused. He gazed around the field, seeing his soldiers falling. Many of them are already dead. He turned to Yabel and gaze toward his aduroblade. Amten raised his head toward the sky, calling out the Sinstorian gods to assist him in battle. He received not an answer. He hanged his head and nodded.

"If they won't aid me, I'll do it myself."

Amten went to impale Yabel with his blade. Yabel moved out of his way and swiped his aduroblade across Amten's back. The armor shattered from the strength of the swing. Amten fell to the ground. Yabel stood over him and kneeled down before him.

"Only if your Pharao had listened to our warnings, you would still be in Misriayim right now and your soldiers would be intact."

"Do not speak ill of the Pharao. He will get what he desires."

"And what does he desire from us?"

"He seeks to find the Grail."

"The Grail?" Yabel said. "What Grail?"

"The Grail that is said to possess the power to give its wielder the might to overtake any nation they seek."

"Where is the location of this Grail?"

Amten started to fade away. Yabel wasn't having it,

shaking the near-dead Governor in an attempt to keep him awake for a few more seconds.

"Tell me where the location is?"

Amten said not a word and died from the wounds. Yabel hung his head and stood up. He nodded toward Amten's body and walked away, returning to the Rayen and the Knights. Making his return, he noticed they had won the battle. The Knights cheer their victory, giving The High One the glory. Yabel approached Rayen.

"I see we've won this battle."

"Yes we have. What of their leader? The Governor?"

"He is on the other side now." Yabel said.

"Wonder what the Elders will say concerning this battle."

"You and me both."

The Knights gather what they can as the spoils of war and leave the planet of Thran, returning to Helio.

In returning to Helio, the Knights enter the city of Tropolton. Hearing the cheers from the residents as they make way toward the Temple of the Avior. Inside the temple stood Elder Knight Iscar. Iscar greeted the Knights on their return. Yabel and Rayen entered the temple with hugs from Iscar down to everyone else, including the Knights.

"I can already sense you've won the battle against the Sinstorians." Iscar said. "Well done, Knight Commanders."

"Thank you, Elder." Yabel said. "We did what we could at our best."

"That I can fully see." Iscar said with a nod. "I am sure you're all tired from the battle. I suggest you all gather some rests. You deserve it."

The Knights leave the temple except for Yabel and Rayen.

"It is wonders to see two Knight Commanders succeed in a battle like this. Not many have done the same mind you."

"We understand very well, Elder." Rayen said. "Perhaps

someday, we will teach those after us these manners in order to continue such a strong way.”

“That is the goal, Knight Rayen.”

Iscar hugged both Knights as they left the temple. Each Knight returned to their own homestead. Yabel entered his home, seeing his wife Ashona, her handmaiden Ila, and his son Sephor, who is now at the age of five. Sephor ran to his father. Yabel picked up his son with happiness as Ashona approached him.

“You have returned to us.” She said.

“Yes I have. The battle was great and we overcame the Sinstorians.”

“The Avior was with you.”

“Indeed it was.”

“Father.” Sephor said.

“Yes, my son?”

“Can I go along with you next time?”

“I don’t think you’re ready for that field yet, Sephor. Perhaps when you grow older, you’ll be there with me.”

“How old must I be to go out and fight?”

“Old enough.” Yabel said with certainty.

Sephor nodded with a faint smile. Yabel smiled back as he kissed his son on the head and placed him back on his feet. Yabel enjoyed the time with his wife and son. He was also considering to take Ila for a second wife, but the agreement had yet to be made.

Later that night, Yabel returned to the temple to speak with Iscar concerning the words spoken by Amten. Meeting Iscar in his study. Iscar was eager to see Yabel. He could sense something within him.

“What is it you have this time?”

"During the battle, I faced their leader. Amten, he was one of their Governors. Before he died, he told me the Pharao was seeking some grail."

"A grail?"

"Yes. I don't know what he was speaking about. It seemed strange to me. I was asking you to see if you may know anything of this."

"I know about a grail, Knight Yabel. One in particular."

"What is it?"

Iscar walked over to one of the bookshelves and searched. Finding the book he was looking for, he grabbed it and laid it on the table. Opening the book, turning through the pages, he stopped and pointed. Yabel looked.

"Is that what he was speaking of, Elder?"

"It is." Iscar said. "They call it the Lost Grail."

"Lost?"

"Lost meaning hidden in their vocabulary. The Grail was once wielded by the Knights Regiar, a sect of knights that reigned over the planet Kuward."

"I've never known about those knights."

"Not many have. Most of them were eliminated during their war with what they call 'The Evil One'."

"The Evil One being who we know for sure?"

"The Fallen One. He figured to make war with the Knights Regiar and another sect on Kuward. Causing a civil war amongst the planet. They ended up destroying one another till there was hardly anything or anyone left. It is a blessing that Ashona was not harmed in that conflict."

"And that conflict is what created the Thunder Knight?"

"Yes. Now, tell me, why do you ask of this Grail?"

"Just as I did with the fountain on Kuward. I seek to find it and bring it here for protection from our enemies and those of carnal minds."

"If you were granted permission to find this Grail, I hope you won't succumb to the same fate as with your search for the fountain."

"I believe I will not make that same mistake, Elder."

Iscar nodded as he closed the book. He turned to Yabel.

"I will have an answer in the morning. Let me speak with another Elder to get a better clearance on this subject."

Yabel nodded with respect and left Iscar's study. Iscar left his study sometime after Yabel, making his way into the other side of the temple. Sitting on the other end is a room, detailed as any room would be. Except this room is filled with the anointing of the Avior. It humbled Iscar as he made it way into the room. Sitting in a chair within the room is another Elder. Older than Iscar. Much older. Iscar bowed before him.

"Elder, may I have a word?"

The older Elder was dressed in a white robe and his head was covered with a hood. He raised his head, facing Iscar. The older Elder is Ocha. the oldest Knight and the oldest man in all of Tropolton and Helio. Possibly older than anyone else in the sector. Ocha is full of wisdom. The wisdom is like flowing water within Ocha's being as his aura glows white, signifying a complete bond with the Avior.

"You seek to ask me of allowing Yabel to find the Grail?"

"Yes. He is keen on discovering it and bringing it here for safekeeping."

"The Grail is a powerful weapon. Its power even rivals the Parcels of Arkkon when it comes to whomever possesses it."

"But, I have not forgotten what happened to him on his last journey out into the universe alone."

"I am aware of your concern for Yabel's protection of his spirit. I am aware. As is The High One. Yet, do not worry. The Avior will keep Yabel in line."

"Are we sure it can? We know the struggle his father had

with the Avior and the Dekar?”

“Yabel is not Lysander.” Ocha declared. “Yabel is far stronger within the Avior than his father. I can speak of this.”

“Elder Ocha, I ask you, what is your solution to this matter? Should Yabel go out and retrieve the Grail or should he abandon this journey?”

Ocha nodded and prayed to The High One. Speaking in the Aviorian tongue. He prayed and waited for a few seconds. After those seconds had passed and opened his eyes and looked at Iscar.

“Command the main Knights to accompany Yabel on this journey. To see if their ally is intact with the Avior and not pulled by the Dekar.”

“Is this what you suggest to be the best solution?”

“Yes. Rayen knows Yabel more than the other Knights. He will watch out for his friend.”

“I will inform them of this, Elder.” Iscar said as he bowed once more before leaving the room.

In the morning, Iscar informed Yabel of the decision and told him to rally up the Knights to join him. Yabel understood the words spoken by Ocha to Iscar. Yabel respected them completely. He went out of the temple and gathered the Knights. Telling them to prepare for a travel to Kuward, the last known location of the Grail. Rayen was prepared as were the Knights. Yabel said his goodbyes to his wife and son as he and the Knights flew off to Kuward.

II
THE KUWARDIAN KNIGHT

The Knights left Helio, making their way to Kuward in the sector of Star 114. The Helio-Sor ships traveled at stellar speed, making a faster pace to reach Kuward. Yabel gives the details of the mission to the Knights. All but Rayen was aware of the matter at hand. Yabel knew he could trust his friend with the utmost information needed. Many of the Knights were just Knights. Only Yabel and Rayen were high-ranking Knights on the mission. The Elder Knights remained on Helio to oversee other details coming from across the sectors, primarily keeping an eye on their enemies seeking to take Helio from them.

"Once we reach Kuward, where do we go?" Rayen asked Yabel.

"We won't make landfall near the castle." Yabel said. "It would be best to make landing near the wilderness. This Grail we're after, its hidden on the planet and I know for certain it is not kept within the castle. I would've come across it otherwise. Ashona would've told me of its existence."

"Did she know about the Grail?"

"She did. She's the one who told me to search the wilderness. She believes the protectors of the Grail kept it there. Away from those who would come to the planet seeking it."

"Like ourselves." Rayen said with a smile.

"Yeah. Like ourselves."

Within the flash of light, the ships bolt through the

stellarspeed and are approaching Kuward. Yabel tells the Knights to prepare for landing. The ships enter Kuward's atmosphere and make their way toward the wilderness. An area on Kuward surrounded by trees and mountains.

"Prepare for landing." Yabel said.

The ships find an open spot near the wilderness and make their landings. The Knights exit the ships and rally together with Yabel and Rayen up front. They scout the wilderness, seeing nothing but trees ahead.

"We just enter the forest?" Rayen said. "Or do we make a wait?"

"We enter the forest, my brother." Yabel said. "Only way to know for sure what lies inside."

Yabel and Rayen walk toward the forest as the Knights follow them. Upon making their steps, from the forest bolted out a knight dressed in Kuwardian armor. Similar to the Thunder Knight's armor, but in different colors. The colors of red, gold, and silver. The man raised up his sword, made of Kuwardian steel toward Yabel and Rayen. The Knights halted and reached for their aduroblades. Yabel and Rayen did the same.

"Who are you and why have you come to trespass this land?" The knight asked.

"We are the Knights of the Covenant. Servants to The High One." Yabel said. "Those of the Avior."

The knight nodded, but he didn't lower his sword. He took a keen eye toward the Knights behind Yabel and Rayen.

"You came with a lot. Why have you come?"

"We're looking for something called the Lost Grail."

"No." The knight said. "You're not taking it from here!"

The knight went to strike Rayen, who was set for a fight. He held his aduroblade tightly. Its glowing white blade with its golden aura intimidated the knight. He isn't aware of such weaponry.

"What kind of blade do you people possess?"

"Aduroblades." Rayen said. "Made from the minerals of the universe. Replicas of the Celestials' own."

The knight also stared at Yabel's aduroblade. The green blade glowing with a white aura. He also saw the Knights behind them with their own aduroblades. Ranging from made blade colors and auras.

"I'm sure they won't have the might of a Kuwardian blade."

The knight swiped his blade against Yabel's own. Yabel kept still as Rayen went to strike the knight. The knight dodged Rayen's swirls before colliding his blade with Rayen's. Yabel made his move and elbowed the knight in the head before Rayen tripped him to the ground. The two Knight Commanders stood over the knight with their blades near his neck.

"We did not come here to fight." Yabel said. "Tell us who you are?"

"Why should I do so?"

"Because we told you who we are." Rayen said. "Best to be respectful."

The knight nodded and held his hand up. The Knight Commanders removed their aduroblades from the knight's neck. He stood up, rubbing his head. And placing his own blade into its sheath, which sat upon his back.

"What is your name, knight?" Yabel asked.

"My name is Galahad.' The knight said. "I am a member of the Knights Regiar. Protectors of House Pendragon and servants of the great Arturus, the Kuwardian King."

"Arturus?" Rayen said. "I've heard of that name before."

"Where?" Yabel asked.

"During one of the battles against the Ordowians on

Zappdow. One of the wizards spoke of a king named Arturus. Said he died in battle protecting his home.”

“Is that the truth?” Yabel asked Galahad.

“I am not aware of my king’s whereabouts. I was only ordered to remain here and to protect the Grail for as long as I could.”

“So, you know where the Grail is?”

“I do. A particular location.”

“Where is this location?”

“Why should I tell either of you its location?” Galahad said. “What do the Knights of the Covenant seek to do with the Grail in their possession?”

“We desire to keep it from enemy hands.” Yabel said. “Primarily away from Those of the Dekar.”

“The Dekar.” Galahad murmured. “I’ve heard about those people and the dark power they wield.”

“I take it you’re familiar with them. The Viper Order and their Lords.”

“I am. But, the last time I ever encountered a Viper Lord was during the early reign of my king. When the Viper Lord called Sinth Bane made his arrival to Kuward. He sought an allegiance with my king. But, King Arturus denied the arrangement and the following months came terror in many forms.”

“What forms?” Rayen asked.

“The forms of riders. There were six of them. Shrouded in darkness, but bright as a flame. Their countenance burned with a fervent heat. They smelled of brimphur. They wielded blades such as yours, but they were dark and looked as if they’ve been melted over and over.”

“They’re called Ephruach.” Rayen said.

“You mean those Viperwraiths we dealt with when we were only children?”

"Yeah."

"After their invasions, the Knights Regiar were almost wiped out completely. Only a fee of us managed to survive. Those invasions is what led King Arturus to go to war with the Viper Order."

"And you haven't heard or seen from them since?"

"That is correct, Knight of the Covenant."

Yabel approached Galahad with respect. He nodded with a gesture toward the forest.

"Can you do us a favor. Just one?"

"What kind of favor?"

"Show us the location of the Grail. Let us take it from here and return to Helio. We will have it placed in a room where there are other objects just like it."

"You've all done this before?"

"A few times."

Galahad nodded before facing Yabel, Rayen, and the Knights. He nodded with respect and turned toward the forest.

"Follow me." Galahad said. "Carefully."

They entered the Kuwardian wilderness with Galahad leading them toward the Lost Grail.

III
THE RACE FOR THE GRAIL

Yabel stood next to Galahad as they entered the wilderness. Within the forest, nothing can be seen. Only the sound of the fowls of the air could be heard. The Knights make their movement as quiet as possible, following Galahad.

"How far is this particular location?" Yabel asked.

"The location is not as far as you would believe. We will be led to it."

"How?"

"The Grail will present itself before us and will guide us to its location."

"You've seen this before?" Rayen asked.

"Yes. It guided me to protect it."

The planet Moraltis, sitting in the sector of Star 895. Within the Moraltian Castle sat the Viper Lords, Sinth Julius and Sinth Juliana. Husband and wife of the Viper Order. Cloaked and hooded in their black clothing and their aduroblades kept to the sides of the thrones. The aura of the Dekar fumes from their being. Giving off the aroma of the malevolent power. Both sat on their thrones as a sect of howlshockers, the stealth patrol of the Shocker Troops entered the throne room.

"What news do you have for us?" Julius asked.

"My lord, during our patrol around the sector, Star 114, we discovered a signal coming from Kuward."

"Kuward?" Juliana said. "That desolate place where the Knights Regiar were extinguished?"

"Yes, my Lady. We tracked down the source and found out it is coming from within the wilderness of the planet. Far from the Kuwardian Castle."

"Were you able to get a sight of this source?" Julius asked. "Anything you found of a physical form?"

"No, my Lord. When we made the attempt to enter the planet, we were warded off by some unseen power. It's nothing we've experienced before. It felt strange."

Julius nodded toward the howlshockers.

"Very well." He said. "Gather more of your shockers."

"Yes, my Lord." The Commander said, exiting the throne room.

Julius turned his focus toward his wife, "Juliana, we're going to visit Kuward."

"Why?" She said with confusion. "You could just send the howlshockers back with some of the rainshockers."

"I could. But…"

"But what?"

"I personally need to find out what this source may be. It sounds far too similar to the Parcels of Arkkon. Yet, it may not be so. There is another artifact that it may be."

"What kind of artifact?"

"One that is regularly hidden from prying eyes."

Julius rose up from his throne. Walking toward the doors.

"Best we may a way for the artifact. Otherwise, the Knights of the Covenant will beat us to it."

Yabel, Rayen, and the Knights continue to follow Galahad through the deep wilderness, seeking to find the location of the Lost Grail. Coming upon nothing since entering the wilderness, the Knights are still steady, prepared for any possible attack.

"Just a little further." Galahad said. "The Grail will make itself known to us."

"How does it work?" Yabel asked. "The Grail making itself known."

"It appears when it chooses to. To those who are deemed worthy enough to gaze upon its presence. Not everyone is meant to see the Grail. That is why some have called it the Lost Grail."

"The Sinstorians preferred to call it the Hidden Grail."

"I am aware their language is far different from the Kuwardian tongue."

As they moved deeper, above them appeared a bright light. The Knights paused in their tracks while Yabel, Rayen, and Galahad looked up toward the light. Unaware of what it may be. They each prepared themselves for the possible fight.

"What is that?" Yabel said.

"Wait." Galahad said. "Just wait."

The light inched closer toward them, brightening up the forest. Galahad started deep into the light and what he could see was the Grail itself. It spoke to him in the Kuwardian tongue. Galahad was the only one who could understand the voice of the Grail. Yabel squinted his eyes, looking into the light and he could see the Grail, yet could not understand the language, for it was not known to him, but only known to Galahad.

"What is it saying?"

"The Grail wants us to find it." Galahad said. "And to make it as fast as possible."

"Why make it fast?"

"There are enemies on the way. From both sides of the planet."

"Enemies?" Rayen said. "What kind of enemies."

"The Viper Order." Yabel said. "They must know about the Grail."

Galahad looked up into the light once more. The Grail continuing to speak to him before the light evaporated from the air, leaving the forest as it once was. Galahad turned to the Knights. He nodded to himself. To keep himself focused.

"What is it, Galahad?" Yabel asked.

"The Viper Order aren't the only ones on the way."

"Who else knows about the Grail?"

Nearby a bolt of lighting hit's the forest. Catching the Knights; attention. The trees around them begin to fall to the sides. The entire area turned into a wasteland within mere seconds. Walking through the downed trees and entering the wasteland are a group of men. The men ranged from young to old. Hey wore violet and scarlet cloaks, robs, and hoods. The man leading them was dressed in complete scarlet with hints of violet and he wore a hat over his head. His eyes were the color of a dim light. The Knights know of these men as does Galahad. They are the Magus Court, the clan of wizards from the planet of Ordow. Worshippers of the Lord of the Black Arts. Leading them is the Master Wizard himself.

"Galahad of the Knights Regiar." The Master Wizard said. "You have something that belongs to us."

IV
LEAVE WHAT SHALL BE

"What do I have that belongs to your kind?"

"The Grail. Give it to us. Now."

Galahad stood in between the Knights and the Court. Both sides prepared for a fight.

"You cannot have it." Galahad said. "What good can you and your people do with it?"

"It won't matter to you. You're not one of us. Therefore, hand us the Grail and we will return to Ordow. Peacefully."

"No. You're not getting the Grail."

The Master Wizard nodded. "I see you've made your decision on the matter."

"I have." Galahad said boldly.

The Master Wizard rose his hand toward Galahad, snatching him with the magical abilities he possesses. He held Galahad in his grasp tightly. Galahad is unable to move, shaking his way to find an escape. Yabel raises up his aduroblade and stood before the Master Wizard.

"Let him go."

"Why would I do such a thing?" The Master Wizard asked.

"Because if you harm him, you'll never find out where the Grail is kept."

"A fair point. However, why do you speak to me concerning such a powerful artifact? Anyhow, why are the Knights of the Covenant here on Kuward? What possesses you people to gain this treasure of power?"

"We desire to obtain the Grail to keep it from the likes of our enemies. The Viper Order, the Sinstorians, and those such as yourself."

"I believe that most certainly. You don't intend to take this Grail and use it against your enemies. Especially during this most trying time, dealing with a war to take over your planet and homeland. Which, we will succeed in doing so."

"You Ordowians will never gain Tropolton or Helio." Rayen said. "We will protect our home with all our might and all out spirit."

"I love your passion for your home and for your god." The Master Wizard said. "In time, you will come to the understanding that there is only one mighty power in all the universe and that power is magic itself."

"You ancient fool." Yabel said.

"You dare to call me a fool?"

"I do. Because while we're here on a mission and you've just intervened in our mission. The only way I see either of us getting out of here is one of us lives and the other dies."

The Master Wizard dropped Galahad to the ground. Locking his eyes on Yabel. The Master Wizard's hands glow a dark violet aura. Filled with mystic energy. Yabel held tightly to his aduroblade. Both standing before one another.

"You desire to challenge me to a fight, Knight?"

"If that is what it will take." Yabel said. "And I'm a Knight Commander now. Not just a Knight."

"As if that will protect you from the power I wield."

"I have faith the Avior will grant me all the power I need to defeat you."

"Typical of you Knights of the Covenant. Placing your strength into something unseen."

"Test me to find out if this power is truly unseen, Wizard."

Before they started to fight each other, from the sky

appears an arsenal of fighter ships. The ships of the Viper Order. Galahad watched as the ships made landfall around the forest. Yabel and Rayen were prepared for the double attack they knew was imminent. The leading ship, the Sinth-Tred landed directly in front of the Knights and the Court. The ship opened and out walked Sinth Julius and Sinth Juliana. They stopped in their tracks and started at the opposing forces.

"What do we have here." Julius said. "The Knights and the Wizards all in one place."

"I trust you haven't come here to thwart our arrangement concerning the War of Helio?" The Master Wizard asked Julius with intent.

"I have not. The deal still stands. However, me and my wife have come to this wasted planet to claim something we sorely need in our arsenal."

"What would that be?" Yabel asked.

"The Grail. We know it is here ad it is very close."

"You're not getting the Grail." Galahad declared. "Its power is above your reach."

Julius measured Galahad closely. He noticed his armor and his garments. Pointing at Galahad with interest. He looked over to Juliana and smiled.

"He's one of them."

"One of whom?"

"A member of the Knights Regiar. I didn't know there were any that survived the destruction of your Arturusian Kingdom."

"Not many of us managed to survive the attacks your kind unleashed upon this planet as you have done with many others out in the universe."

"Out of all of us here at this moment, you're the only one with the knowledge to the Grail's location?"

"Yes I am."

"Good." Julius nodded. "Then, you will have no problem leading me and my wife to it."

"You're not getting the Grail, Viper Lord." The Master Wizard said.

"How come I will not?"

"The Grail belongs with the Magus Court. Sorcery can be increased upon the sectors with its power."

"The Grail belongs in the proper hands of protection." Yabel said. "Which is why we're here."

Yabel and Rayen stood together. Side by side. Their blades were raised and prepared for battle. In front of them stood the Magus Court with the Master Wizard armed with the aura circling his hands. Julius and Juliana both pulled out their aduroblades. Galahad backed away as he knew what was about to unfold.

V

VISIONS OF THE COMING

The battle was commenced with the Knights colliding with the Magus Court alongside the rainshockers. While the Knights did battle, Yabel and Galahad ran toward the cavern of the grail's dwelling place. Rayen saw them running for it, he went to follow before Yabel turned back, holding his hand out.

"You're sure?" Rayen asked.

"I'm sure. Keep them away."

Rayen turned around, seeing rainshockers approaching and without hesitation, he swiped them with his aduroblade, cutting them in half from the torso. Sinth Julius looked in the distance as he defeated several Magus Court wizards in quick succession, he saw Yabel and Galahad. He followed by walking, not running. Juliana also followed with him while the rainshockers dealt with the sorcerers and the Knights.

Yabel followed Galahad deeper into the wilderness and once the bushes were out of their sight, they found themselves standing in front of an entrance to the cavern. Galahad sighed. The entrance was large and surrounding it were candles. Candles similar to what would've been placed in the Kuwardian castles. A banner rested atop the entrance with the emblem of the Knights Regiar.

"This is the place."

They entered the cavern as a waterfall fell over the cavern.

Inside, Yabel saw it was decorated with oils, imagery of the Kuwardian kingdoms of the past and the marks of the Knights Regiar. Yabel saw all of it and in his heart felt the presence of idolatry. He stood down, knowing he was back home. For this was a foreign land, under a different set of laws. A place of another culture.

"You stayed in here?" Yabel asked. "Lived in here?"

"For most of this present time, yes. After the kingdom was taken under siege, I had no place to go. My brothers were killed in battle and I was kept to guard the grail from those outside who seek it. But, you, you and your Knights are different. You don't desire to acquire the grail for some personal purpose or political gain. You seek to keep it guarded. Protected."

"It's why I'm here."

Galahad took a look at the grail, signaling for Yabel to come closer. He did and the two stood before the grail. Yabel saw how beautiful it was to the eyes. For it gravitated them to it. Galahad knew it would do this. For it is the reason why the kingdom was taken siege to begin with. Why the wars of Kuward happened. All sought the grail.

"Stand firm." Galahad said.

"Why?"

"The grail is set to reveal something to us both. Something pertaining to a time yet to come."

"How are you certain of this?"

"Trust me."

Yabel shook his head and faced the grail. Galahad did the same and it started to shake. Within the grail busted out a bright essence of light. Its colors were similar to the clear sky, yet with glares of gold, white, and red within it. Galahad and Yabel's eyes were set on the light and in a second, they were pulled into the light. No their bodies, but their spirits. Now, they were within the light and what they saw was a time ahead. They looked and watched as the Viper Order had grown in a time yet to come. Their power was over all the sectors. Yet, in another place amongst the Order's rule was a young man. Galahad froze when he saw him."

"It's him!"

"Who? Who's he?" Yabel questioned.

The young man was seen in the light facing the Order and defeating them. Also in this light, the young man wielded an aduroblade of his own and was facing off against a Viper Lord. One that has never been seen before. He appeared as if he was the embodiment of the Dekar. Yet, the young man was seen to appear as the embodiment of the Avior. The young man defeated the Viper Order and liberated the sectors from their rule. Galahad sighed and they were dropped back into their bodies as the light evaporated from the air, returning to the grail.

"You saw all of that?" Galahad asked.

"I did." Yabel said. "I saw everything."

"Now, I understand. I know what I must do now."

Galahad reached for the grail, but he was caught off guard by Julius and Juliana. Both were accompanied by six rainshockers. Their ranges set on Yabel and Galahad. Prepared to fire when commanded. Yabel held his aduroblade steady, ready for the fight. Galahad grabbed his sword and was set to protect the grail at any cost.

VI
A FITTING END

"I suggest you hand it over." Julius said. "Save yourself from a terrible death."

"I will not give you the Grail. Your kind do not deserve it. Nor the power it holds."

"And who are you to tell us what we deserve?" Juliana said. "You are a Knight of a fallen kingdom. You have no authority anymore. Just a shell of an ancient cause."

The rainshockers stood still, ranges armed. Yabel twirled his aduroblade and looked toward Galahad. Julius and Juliana held their blades in hand.

"No need to do this." Yabel said. "Walk away and we can speak of this another day."

"You know our way, Covenant one. We don't walk away. We take and we conquer."

"FIRE!" Julius yelled.

The ranges went off, blasting toward Yabel and Galahad. The blasts ricocheted across the cavern from Yabel's deflecting, some colliding with rainshockers who fired them and ones who did not. Yabel called for the Viper Lords to approach and they did with speed, slamming the blades across Yabel's own. Galahad jumped in, facing Juliana as Yabel held back Julius from the Grail. Julius shoved Yabel back and Yabel pulled Julius away from the Grail and slammed him into the rocked walls.

While the fighting was ongoing, the other Knights entered the cavern and joined in to help their brother and Galahad.

The numbers were too great for the Viper Lords and they stood back. Juliana screamed in anger before stabbing Galahad in the chest with her aduroblade. Yabel turned his blade and collided with Juliana's, in turn, Julius placed his in front, looking into Yabel's eyes.

"This isn't over." Julius said.

"I know." Yabel replied, shoving the Viper Lord from his gaze.

The Viper Lords backed out of the cavern with the Knights in their presence. Once they were gone, the Knights gathered the Grail, prepared to head back to Helio. Galahad laid on the ground with Yabel and Rayen sitting next to him.

"We can heal you." Yabel said. "Come back with us."

"No. no need. I have done my duty and will die as a Regiar. For we both have seen the future and I am content in that fact. I will speak out one thing, a prophecy. I shall return when the *Royal Savior…* is born."

With those words, Galahad took his last breath and gave up the spirit. The two Knights buried Galahad in the cavern where the Grail once rested. They left Kuward and returned to Helio with the Grail in tow. Galahad will be remembered and if his words are correct, he will return. One day.

AMRAN,
THE PRINCE OF SINSTOR
THE RISE OF A PRINCE IN THE *EVER WAR* UNIVERSE

675 BOC
675 YEARS DURING THE *BATTLE OF CAELUM*

"A PRINCE THE PLANET NEEDED. A PRINCE THE WAR CALLED."

THE YOUNG PRINCE

Amran-Em-Of was born in Misriaym on Sinstor in the year 741 BoC to Pharao Sebek-Em-Of during the early period of the War of Helio. Amran grew over the years, learning of the universe around him. The concepts of war and duty intrigued his mind, even at such a young age. The rules of Sinstor were primarily clear of refusing those of a young mind of entering high authoritative positions unless demanded by the Pharao himself. Easy to be of the case, Amran was brought into political meetings and council sessions concerning Sinstor's place in the universe. Amran was guided and taught by the priests of Sinstor and the rules of the Sinstorian gods. Amran primarily gave obeisance to Xanthou, the chief Sinstorian god.

During the War of Helio, Sinstor was at war with Helio and the Knights of the Covenant. One meeting Amran attended concerned Sinstor's place amongst the War of Helio and the potential for taking the planet as their own. Its resources and position intrigued the council. However, Pharao Sebek had other ideas in place for Helio if they were able to conquer it. Sebek told his son that if the time ever came up to where they had to travel to Helio in order to take it and win the war they would do so without question. Amran himself was trained in fighting techniques at the age of seven. A duty to Sinstorian service under Sebek's Dynastic Magocracy.

Within the year 719 BoC, Amran was brought out as one of the Knights of the Covenant came to Sinstor looking for his newly wife. The Knight's presence in the court attracted strong attention especially since I was in the middle of a war between their nations. For a Knight to make himself known and step into the presence of the opposing nation's court gave Sebek much respect, something Amran would learn later in his life. The Knight was demanded to face a Sinstorian of value, Sebek had an option to choose Knight Rayen Grake's opponent and chose Amran as Rayen's opponent. Unsure of his skill, Amran combated Rayen and lost. However, Rayen spared the young prince's life, proclaiming he had a brighter future and would be a better Pharao than his father.

Years later, Amran watched as the Sinstorian armies would be rallied out into the stellarspace to combat the Knights of the Covenant and their allies as the War of Helio intensified. Sebek began to fear for his life and his rule as another threat posed itself across the sectors. Ultimately making their way toward Sinstor and hardly an army to protect him.

The year 680 BoC saw the fall of Sebek's reign as Sultan Nasir-Ah of Assracyia conquered all of Sinstor and gave Sebek the choice of life or death. Sebek's harden pride refused to live under Nasir's rule. Nasir gave his men the signal to kill Sebek, but allowing Amran to live. Nasir had a liking to the young prince. The Dynastic Magocracy of Sebek's rule ended with his death and gave rise to Nasir's Ayyubid Dynasty of Sinstor. Amran lived under Nasir's rule and gave much respect to the first Sinstorian Sultan.

THE YOUNG QUEEN

The city of Magnesia was a place on the planet Ellada kept quiet. Magnesia was formed during the reign of Men upon Ellada and left abandoned after the separation period. Livia, born the same years as Amran, a young woman stumbled upon the old city during a walk and claimed it for herself. Streaked brown hair, green eyes, and a bold countenance, she gathered an army of women warriors and star horses and chariots. She began trade deals with other nations in other sectors. Gaining wealth from the trade deals, she proclaimed herself Queen Livia of Magnesia and quickly became an adversary to Queen Herena of Olympya.

Their wars would be ongoing until Livia learned of the War of Helio. The change for greater fame and wealth seduced her mind and she left Ellada with her army in search of the other nations. Learning by their craft, cultures, and religions and tribes, she kept her mind close to the things that grabbed her attention. The war itself was causing uproar across the sectors. Nations rallying up their own armies in case of a sudden attack. Livia herself decided if the attacks would be done, she would be an attacker not a victim.

On Ellada, Livia was a hated woman amongst those outside the perimeters of Magnesia. However, within the city, she was worshipped as a goddess of war. One who would spill blood before giving glory and honor to another ruler. Her people feared her with respect and honor. The other sectors and nations within them were not aware of Livia's existence and that gave her the ultimate opportunity to strike whenever deemed necessary.

ONE STRIKE

On a day in which they did not see, Queen Livia and her armies arrived on Sinstor. Their first target was the small city of Gubla. The people of Gubla fled in terror of Livia's attack. For example, her army of women warriors sparked confusion amongst the people. Known in Gubla were only male soldiers. Female soldiers were rarely seen in Gubla, even in Sinstor as a whole. The star horses were only another form of terrorizing as they flew over the city with the chariots in tow. Livia commanded the warriors not to kill the civilians, as they were not the cause of her sudden appearance.

"I, Queen Livia of Magnesia, have come before you this day. Not to kill, pillage, or destroy. But to summon your leader. The one who has taken the throne of this planet. For I am aware of your previous Pharao and his death. I have come to seek out this leader from another land. This Nasir-Ah."

Livia informed the people of more details and rallied a few of them to travel to Misriaym to alert Nasir-Ah of her presence. After a few days, Nasir received the news and immediately wanted to meet this Elladian queen. Nasir gathered his men and rode off to Gubla to meet with Livia. Amran, however, was told by Nasir to stay at the palace and not to come out to the meeting. For his own safety.

IV
DECLARATION OF WAR

Nasir-Ah and his men arrived in Gubla and met with Queen Livia, guarded by her warriors as the star horses and chariots flew over the field. The field was covered with lilies. Their height was near above the wrists. Nasir kept a clear focus, seeing someone from another nation in his presence, one of royalty at most.

"Why have you invaded my land?" Nasir questioned.

"You speak of invasion and yet, isn't that what you have done."

"I did what was best for the Sinstorian people and my own. Pharao Sebek-Em-Of was an unruly man and I freed all the people of his sovereignty. What have you done in order to become a queen yourself?"

"I took my place. That is what I am. I take and I conquer."

"You seek to conquer Sinstor?" Nasir questioned harshly. "Is that why you've arrived and have terrorized my people?"

"I am no longer welcomed home on my world. I have decided to find others suitable for my desires. This place you call Sinstor, I see is filled with such luxury. A little rustic to my taste, but, luxurious."

"You cannot have Sinstor. This planet is under my

rule. Under my dynasty.”

“I’m not departing until I have this place under my rule.”

“You wish not to leave on your own will?”

“I do not.”

“Very well, I suggest you pray to your gods, Queen Livia of Magnesia and ask them for a quick deliverance. For in three days time, you will need it.”

“We shall see.”

Nasir and his men rode off back to Misriaym. Meanwhile, Livia and her warriors dwelled in Gubla. The people treated her like a queen unless they sought to die by the blades and spears of her warriors. When Nasir returned to the palace, he informed all who were present of what occurred and officially declared war on Queen Livia. He sent out spies to travel to Gubla to quietly inform the people to evacuate as the days approached. In three days time, he would attack.

THE GODS OF SINSTOR VS. THE GODS OF ELLADA

The three days had come and gone. Nasir rode with his army and Sinstorian priests to Gubla to meet with Queen Livia. Nasir chose the strategy of riding out at dawn. As the morning fully came, Livia discovered all the people of Gubla were gone. Only herself and her warriors remained. Livia walked out of the home she was staying and could hear the horses in the distance. There, she saw Nasir and the two thousand men that followed on horseback. They arrived at the city and began in immediate combat with the warriors. The star horses were shot down by arrows.

In the midst of the battle, the Sinstorian priests walked out, fully clothed in white robes with golden lining. Their heads covered as they looked to the sky and began calling out the names of their gods. They called out Xanthou, their creator. Secondly, they called out Apademak, one of their warrior gods to assist in the battle. They also called out Montju, another god of war who was also god of the sun. Montju was called out to keep the sun in its place so Nasir and the army could win the battle. Livia was introduced by the Sinstorian priests and she screamed out with a heavy voice,

"Priests of Oros! I summon you!"

From the home behind her appeared four priests,

dressed in robes that only hung on one shoulder. They also wore sun disks over their heads. They were priests of Ellada. Priest of Mount Oros of the Dodekatheon. Their dress was unfamiliar to the culture of Sinstor. The priests began a summoning bout with the Sinstorian priests. Each called out the gods assonated with their religion and what was present in front of them. Such as the sun, the clouds, the sand, the grass, the water, and the air. The battle lasted for hours and ended with the defeat of Livia's women warriors. Nasir sought to kill the young queen, but he did not.

"A king does not kill a queen." Nasir said to Livia. "For even if the gods of Sinstor aided, Qurlah prevailed."

Nasir commanded Livia to leave Gubla and return to Ellada to face Queen Herena. Nasir and his army burned the bodies of Livia's warriors in honor of a great battle. Some of the bodies that did not burn down completely were brought over to the Yeor Waterlands and were food for the Yeor Dragons, the four-legged scaly beasts of the waters. Their growls can be heard from a great distance.

Livia did leave Gubla and the people returned. However, Livia did not leave Sinstor as she made her way toward Misriaym to confront Nasir once again. For in Livia's mind, only death will permit her exit.

VI
A PRINCE AGAINST A QUEEN

Days later, Nasir and the people of Misrayim celebrated their victory against Queen Livia. They relished in drinking and dancing. Some shouted out the names of the Sinstorian gods in praise. Nasir only credited Qurlah for the victory, for Nasir would never surrender the religion of Laham for the religion of the Mystical Ones. He did have respect toward it. Nasir sat in the throne room with Amran next to him and he told Amran of the events which occurred on the battlefield. As he did, two guardsmen entered the throne room, saying a visitor was present. Nasir allowed the visitor to enter and saw Livia walked through the doors.

He stood up with haste as she walked in and stood in the middle of the room. Amran saw Livia and how young she was. Nasir asked why she didn't leave Sinstor. Livia told him only death would sever her from Sinstorian grounds. Nasir commanded her to turn around and leave at once. She denied to command. After several attempts to get her to leave with her life, he asked her how would she like to die. Livia stated by combat, due to her Elladian heritage. Nasir agreed to the terms and even allowed Livia to choose her opponent. She pointed toward Amran with a grin on her face.

"The Prince of Sinstor." She said.

Nasir did not want Amran to battle Livia. Amran had

told him of his battle in a previous time with a Knight of the Covenant and how he proved himself to his father and those who were in attendance. Nasir brought forth elders who witnessed Amran's battle with the Knight and attested to the account. Therefore, Nasir permitted Amran to combat Livia. Amran grabbed the same weapon he wielded when he faced the Knight. The aureate and staff hybrid. The weapon was unheard of by Ellaidans or Assracyians. Nasir himself was astonished when he saw the glow of the weapon. Livia was intrigued. She wanted one herself.

The two battled it out in the middle of the throne room. The twirls and glow of the axe proved to be a distraction to Livia as she could not fully focus on the fight. She only wielded her sword. The battle itself lasted for an hour with Amran eventually winning as the axe sliced Livia's throat and she fell to the floor and bled to death. The Sinstorians and Assracyians cheered and rallied for Amran's victory. Nasir was proud of the young prince. It presented a different side of Amran to the Sultan of Sinstor.

VII
THE YOUNG PHARAO

Some months after the battle with Queen Livia, the War of Helio was intensifying. To the point where the planet of Assryacia was greatly impacted and the Knights of the Covenant were at a conflict with Ordowians with Sinstor on their radar. Nasir felt he should keep his focus on his home world and assist the people there. In doing so, he turned to Amran and returned the ruler ship to his hands.

"Sinstor is yours now. As it once was, as it is now. Rule well, young Pharao."

Nasir returned the crown to Amran not only because he was the rightful heir to the throne, but because he was like a son to Nasir himself. Amran was now the Pharao of Sinstor. Nasir and all that pertained to him left the planet, returning to Assryacia. Only a few Assryacians remained to assist Amran in his rule. The first step of Amran's rule was to transform Sinstor into a new dynasty. A New Kingdom.

<u>LORDS OF THE VIPER</u>

435 BOC
435 YEARS DURING THE *BATTLE OF CAELUM*

<u>I</u>
CONQUERORS

"Serve The Fallen One and spread the Dekar across all nations." - Empress Venefica

Sinth Zane and Sinth Sahara, the Lords of the Viper Order, both powerful in the knowledge and power of the Dekar, husband and wife. The two together have made a conquest of traveling through the universe, collecting resources and knowledge that would prove use to them and the Viper Order. Making claim to planets and sectors in the universe at a powerful rate, pouring fear upon those who hate them and despise their philosophy. Now, after taking a claim out of their war against the Herenian Empire, Zane and Sahara have reached their point of climax. Both prepared themselves for their final breaths before entering the realm of the Dekar. Before leaving the realm of the living, they have each handpicked two that will become their successors.

A ceremonial event is held within the Moraltian Castle of the Viper Order. The interior of the castle is filled with a sea of rainshockers, howlsoldiers, Imperial Viper Knights, and residents of Moraltis all standing on opposite sides of the walls as the colors of black, red, and gold consume the environment. In the middle of the floor lays a long and extended red carpet, resembling the dark red of the Viper

Lords. Sitting at the end of the carpet are both Zane and Sahara, age had overcome them and their wars of the century has taken its toll on them both. They sat in the seats of the Viper Lords. The front doors of the castle open and two figures enter in, walking atop the dark red carpet. The rainshockers, howlsoldiers, Imperial Viper Knights, and the residents all bow their heads toward the two figures, showing respect and honor to them both.

"Come." Sinth Zane said. "Stand before me and my lady Sahara."

The two figures reached the end of the carpet and stood facing Zane and Sahara. One figure was a man, whom was cloaked in all black with a robe and laced plated armor. A black hood covered his face. The other figure was a woman, dressed in black with a shroud over her face. Both of them bowed and kneeled before Zane and Sahara.

"The time has come." Zane said. "For the change of the air has spoken it and the Dekar allows it."

Zane approached the man and touched his shoulder and he rose up. Sahara approached the woman and touched her on her shoulder and she rose up. Zane reached toward his side and handed the man an aduroblade as did Sahara with the woman. Zane walked over toward a table that stood near the seats. Laying atop the table was the Sinthblade, which is passed down to every Viper Lord throughout the generations. Zane handed the Sinthblade to the man. The man and woman both turned toward each other, looking at one another in the eyes.

"Do the two of you agree to stand side by side in all your works for the glory of the Dekar?"

"We do." The man and woman said.

"Man, do you agree to give the proper orders and instructions to those below your rank and make sure they excel in their works given to them in the glory of the Dekar?"

"I do."

"Woman, do you agree to stand by your husband and obey all that he has to speak toward you and your works?"

"I do."

"Man, do you swear upon the Lord of the Dekar that you will remain faithful to him, to the Viper Order, and to your wife?"

"I do."

"Woman, do you swear to love your husband above all the things within the realm we live in and serve him until your time of calling is at hand?"

"I do."

"The both of you, join arms."

The man and woman joined arms. The man's left arm to the woman's right arm. Within the middle of them stood the Sinthblade, which was in the left hand of the man. Zane commanded them to raise up their arms above them.

"This day, I, Sinth Zane, proclaim the two of you to be henceforth known as Sinth Tyrannus and Sinth Labara. This day, the two of you are crowned as the new Viper Lords of the Order!"

The audience applauded with cheers and yelling. Tyrannus and Labara approached the two seats and place themselves within them, Zane standing next to Tyrannus as did Sahara stand next to Labara. The rainshockers held up their right arms forward, the howlshockers held up their left arms forward, the Viper Knights held up their aduroblades and they all chanted the names of Tyrannus and Labara.

After the ceremony a reception was held within the walls of the Moraltian Castle with residents drinking and partying with each other in celebration of the new crowned Viper Lords. Tyrannus and Labara both attended the party as they sat together at the Viper Lord table with Zane and Sahara sitting with them.

"We chose the both of you for a reason." Zane said. "That being said, we fully believe that the Dekar will truly empower the two of you to do more wonders than we ever could."

"We did our part in the conquering." Sahara said. "Now, it is your turn to do such a task. Make us, the Viper Order, and the Lord of the Dekar proud in all of your deeds in his service."

"Lastly, let the power of the Dekar surge through your being. Let its power show you true knowledge and understanding. With it, the two of you will be able to do and accomplish anything of your heart's desires."

Standing against the walls within the reception are the rainshockers, howlsoldiers, and Viper Knights. Keeping guard of the room and the entrances. Tyrannus and Labara stood up from the Viper Lord table and exited the room. Everyone within the room kneeled down and bowed before them. Chanting their names in the glory of the Dekar. Walking down the corridor, lighted up with fire and the moonlight, Tyrannus and Labara enter their chambers, where their ceremonial bed awaited them as they knew the laws of being crowned Viper Lords. They understood the tasks require for such a position of power.

"I want to see your face." Tyrannus said, removing Labara's shroud from her face and gazing at her beauty, which was shown through her eyes and features.

The two of them both laid down upon the ceremonial bed and desired one another in the ways they pleased. They pleased each other for the entire night, ceasing to run out of energy. That night, Tyrannus and Labara, the new Viper Lords had become one flesh and one in the Dekar.

$\underline{\text{II}}$
ORDER REBORN

When the sun had risen upon Moraltis, after the ceremonial event of the yesterday, Sinth Zane and Sinth Sahara had gave up the ghost that night and died in their bed. The news had went throughout all of Moraltis and later was caught throughout the universe. Even the Knights of the Abhdi had received word of the deaths of the Viper Lords. All of the nations and planets received the news. Some took is with sadness and grief. Some took the news with joy and celebration. Some received the news with mystery and planning. Their funeral had taken place within the Moraltian Castle and their bodies were placed in a marble-like casket made from the molten grounds of Moraltis and they were laid to rest in the Fields of the Viper, where many of the previous Viper Lords are kept buried.

Sinth Tyrannus sat in the chair of the throne room. His head was hanged low as he mourned the death of his mentor. Sinth Labara sat next to him in her chair, she also grieved the death of her mentor. From the throne room doors entered a lieutenant rainshocker, who approached the mourning Viper Lords.

"Sorry to disturb you, my lords."

"What do you have for us, lieutenant?" Tyrannus said.

"The deaths of our previous Lords have spread throughout the universe. Many of the nations and planets are giving out their reception towards their deaths."

"What of their receptions?" Labara said. "How are the nations handling it?"

"The Sinstorians are grieving, the Abhdi Knights are just, the Ordowians are plotting they've said, the Dagobarians are too busy to respond, and the Herenian Empire is shouting for joy and having a celebration."

"The Elladians." Tyrannus said. "Them!"

"What of the Elladians, beloved?"

"They're responsible for our mentors' deaths. Their planet of Ellada was our mentors' last attempt at conquering a planet for our Order. They failed in the task due to interference from the Abhdi Knights and their prized warrior called Serkelrod."

"We appreciate the news, lieutenant. You may leave us."

"Yes, my lords." The lieutenant said, leaving the throne room.

Tyrannus stood up from the chair and walked towards the window behind them, he gazed out towards the fields of Moraltis, witnessing those walking through its green and yellow grounds as well as gazing at the graves of those who came before him and his rule. Labara slowly approached him, hugging him from behind.

"What are you plotting out?"

"Our mentors failed in conquering Ellada from the Herenian Empire. I say, we should finish what they started. Let us lead our armies to Ellada and conquer their planet and claim everything there our own. What of a better way to make our mentors and our Lord proud."

"I am with you with whatever you desire, beloved. But, how will we handle the possible interference of the Abhdi

Knights or the Cavaliers?"

"They have yet to feel our power, my love. The Dekar flows through us much more than our mentors. With its power in our hands, we can wipe out the Knights of the Covenant and the Emerald Cavaliers from the universe. Make it clean once more."

"I love when you speak in such a manner."

"First, we'll have to rally up our soldiers. Prepare them for the journey. Meanwhile, you and I will have to acquire a hunter to our advantage."

"Anyone you had in mind, beloved?"

"There is a man whom I've heard about that scouts the universe. Hunt after hunt he roams and receives his rewards in completing his missions. His name is Jakah Pen, the universe's best bounty hunter. So he is called."

"I will get right onto it."

Labara exited the throne room while Tyrannus walked away from the window and near a shrine that was built within the throne room. The shrine is a marble-like statue of their Lord, the one whom is said to have spread the Dekar through the universe. The statue had remnants of what their Lord happened to look like. From his great physique to his wings and to his features. The statue stood tall in the face of Tyrannus, who bowed down before it. His head bowed as well.

"My Lord, my Master, my Mighty One, we will need your guidance and strength for the tasks that stand before us. Show me the power as you've shown my mentor and my fathers before me. Show me and my wife the power of the Dekar. The power that you spread across the universe for those who wish to possess it. We wish to make you proud and to exalt you above our own selves. For we are nothing but fleshly beings walking amidst a planet that the first enash never touched. We were made of the ground, but you were made of the fire.

Please, I ask of you, give us an inch of that fire you were created and formed in. give us that fire and through it, the Dekar will be evermore stronger and powerful than it was before."

Tyrannus stood up and walked from the statue, also leaving the throne room. A low humming sound was coming from the statue, as if something was embedded within its marble feature.

Labara had made the call and from the skies of Moraltis, came down a ship. The ship was silver and blue, almost the shape of a rectangle, but with an end similar to a circle. The ship made its landing and walking out of its hangar doors was Jakah Pen, covered in his light gray armor and his face hidden within his light gray and blue helmet. Jakah was guided by two rain shockers, who lead him toward the throne room. Approaching the room, the two hooded guards opened the door for Jakah to enter, as he entered, he could see Tyrannus and Labara sitting down in the chairs, facing him.

"You've called to see me, Viper Lords?" Jakah said with a muffled voice.

"It is of a very importance." Tyrannus said.

Jakah walked toward them and kneeled before them. Showing his respect and honor. He arose and faced the newly Viper Lords. Tyrannus and Labara measured Jakah from his stance and the weapons that were placed around his armored body.

"You surely come prepared." Labara said.

"I am always prepared for a mission. What mission do you have of me to proceed?"

"We will need you to assist us in invading the planet of Ellada. The home of the Herenian Empire. We seek to wipe them out completely and claim their home as one of our own."

"You seek to eliminate the Elladians from the universe? I like the mission already."

"Though, there is a catch to this mission of ours."

"What catch?"

"The invasion will be in several years time."

"How many years are you talking?"

"An estimated amount of thirty-five years."

"Thirty-five years until you invade? That's your mission?"

"There is a prime reason for the time span of our mission. Our rainshockers aren't fully prepared for the might of their female warriors and their Princess. They need proper training and I was hoping you would give it to them."

"You're giving me the opportunity of training rainshockers. Plus invading Ellada?"

"That is what we're offering to you, Jakah. So, what will be your answer?"

"My answer is simple. I'm in. just, what will I be rewarded with, if I may ask of it."

"The spoils of victory. Whatever your eyes look upon and desire shall be yours to have."

"Anything my eyes lust after will be mine to have. That's what you're telling me?"

"It is. Whatever you so desire."

"I am honored of this, Viper Lords. I will train your rainshockers and turn them into primary soldiers with heightened skills. They'll be different than any other armies you may have seen in your young lifetime. When the time comes, I will assist you in conquering Ellada and putting an end to their Herenian Empire."

Jakah bowed and left the throne room. Tyrannus turned to Labara with a smile on his face as he pulled back his black hood from over his face.

"Our plan is going as we hoped it would." Tyrannus said.

"Jakah will train our shockers and when the thirty-five year line ends, we will invade their world and destroy them from the universe."

"And what of the Knights or the Cavaliers?"

"They will feel the might of our rainshockers, Jakah's abilities, and our power of the Dekar."

They kissed one another before leaving the throne room and entering their chambers to revel in their love with one another.

III
OLYMPYA CONQUEST
400 YEARS DURING THE BATTLE OF CAELUM

The thirty-five years have passed since the agreement was made between the Viper Lords and Jakah Pen concerning the invasion of Ellada. Jakah stayed on Moraltis and trained the thousands of rainshockers and even the howlsoldiers that attended the training sessions. He taught them the arts of hunting, fighting, swordsmanship, hand-to-hand combat, amongst other feats fit for warfare. Tyrannus and Labara spoke with their council detaining the route to Ellada and the easiest way to enter the planet without being spotted by the watchers of the air.

"How are we able to reach Ellada without being spotted in their skies?" said a member of the Council.

"We shouldn't have to worry about them noticing us before we land." Tyrannus said. "They will see us when we land."

"Are you sure that's an intelligent plan, my lord?"

"It is when I have spoken it."

The Council members turned to each other. Their eyes and facial expressions showing the possibility of fear in their spirits as they look at Tyrannus and Labara. They bow before them, leaving the council room.

"Send word out to Jakah." Tyrannus said. "Tell him to rally up the rainshockers for Ellada."

"I will do so, beloved."

Outside of the castle, Labara approached Jakah, as he stood with the rainshockers and howlshockers. Jakah nodded before Labara. She gazed out at the rainshockers and turned toward the howl soldiers. She smiled as she faced Jakah.

"I can sense they are ready for the battle ahead."

"They have been trained to the highest possibilities, your highness." Jakah said. "I see that you have some news to tell me? Are we preparing to head out toward Ellada?"

"That is why I'm out here. Sinth Tyrannus has sent me to tell you to rally up the rainshockers for takeoff."

"So, we're going to Ellada?"

"That we are doing, Jakah." Labara spoke. "Rally them up and prepare them for the travel ahead."

"I will do so."

All of the Viper Order prepared themselves for the travel toward Ellada. Tyrannus and Labara grabbed their gear and their aduroblades. The rainshockers and howlshockers all gathered together into the Attonbitus with Jakah entering his own ship. From the castle doors, come out Tyrannus and Labara. Prepared and ready for the battle. They enter the Sinth-Tred and as soon as its doors shut, the engines begin to roar. Jakah's ship is already hovering in the air, awaiting the Sinth-Tred and Attonbitus to do the same.

The Sinth-Tred lifted into the air and took off, with Jakah and the Attonbitus following. Within mere seconds, they are out of Moraltis and its atmosphere. The ships are now flying through the stellar space, mapping out the precise location on Ellada to make their landfall. Jakah communicates with Tyrannus and Labara through his helmet. They can hear him talking through the holographic monitors on the ship.

"Which way will we make landfall?" Jakah asked.

"We will land right in the heart of their city of Olympya. There, we will spread out and take the battle to them."

"Understood."

The ships flew past the planets of Sinstor and Ivil, making their exit out of the Star 895 sector and outward into the deep stellar space. Tyrannus looked out and he could mostly see all the planets. Each in sectors. Labara looked out as well, gazing at the amount of worlds that are out in the universe.

"Soon, Labara, we will have in our possession each and every one of these worlds."

"On that day, we will certainly be rulers over the universe."

"That, my wife, is the ultimate goal of the Viper Order."

The ships flew through the deep stellarspace. Passing by other sectors in the universe as they reach for Sector 333, where Ellada is located. Once they arrive toward the sector, the ships slowly make their entrance. Seeing the other planets around them such as Erets-Alpha, Helio, Endro, Endor, Tekh, and Shenxia.

"I see the home of out adversaries, beloved." Labara said, pointing out toward the planet of Helio, the home of the Ancient Knights of the Covenant.

"In time, we will overcome them." Tyrannus said in a calm voice. "In time."

Their ships approached Ellada. Tyrannus and Labara are prepared, just as Jakah and the large amount of rainshockers in the Attonbitus. The ships enter the Elladian atmosphere and they enter the skies over the Elladian cities. Tyrannus looked out, seeing the city of Olympya.

"There!" He yelled. "Land this ship right in the heart of their city!"

The Sinth-Tred Aeronaut proceeded to make the landfall

in Olympya. Jakah's ship and the Attonbitus followed their landing movements. Meanwhile, on the grounds of Olympya, residents to the city gaze up into the air, seeing the three ships approaching. Most of them yell and scream in fear.

"The Viper Order has come!!!" Yelled out a woman holding her daughter by the arm.

From the Temple of Oros, walked out Herena, Queen of the Herenian Empire and beside her is her daughter, Savan-Nah, Princess of the Herenian Empire. They look up toward the ship and stand still, awaiting for them to make their landing. Both women are dressed in the battle gear, covered in leathery clothing covered with armor. Their swords are on their sides. No fear is shown on their faces. Only the signs of war.

The ships slowly land with the wind blowing around the city and in the faces of Herena and Savan-Nah. The Attonbitis opened and out runs the army of rainshockers. All in a single-filed line, with the plasma-ranges in hand. Behind them run out the howlsoldiers, with the stealth gear and riot weaponry. Jakah exits his ship, with his plasma-range aimed for Herena. Jakah laughed, seeing Herena standing in front of the temple. The Sinth-Tred opened and out walks Tyrannus and Labara. They approach Herena and Savan-Nah with Jakah and the rainshockers following them.

"I see the Viper Order has no respects for the residents of others." Herena said.

"We are not here to discuss architecture, woman." Tyrannus said. "We are here to conquer your planet."

"Really? You seek to overthrow me and my empire? So you can take over Ellada?"

"Why else would we be here this day."

Herena turned to Savan-Nah and nodded. Savan-Nah smiled as she pulled up and raised her sword in the air.

"Marvels!" She screamed.

From behind them and around the temple arrive an army of armored-clad women. They are the Marvels of the Universe. The primary army of the Herenian Empire and led by Savan-Nah herself. Tyrannus looked around the landscape, seeing the Marvels around them. Tyrannus turned to Labara and nodded. Labara turned toward the rainshockers.

"Arms up!"

The rainshockers raised up their ranges toward the Marvels. Jakah kept his range steady on Herena. Tyrannus and Herena locked eyes with each other. Knowing the power that both of them possess. Tyrannus pulled out his aduroblade and Sinthblade.

"Let's begin our war, Queen Herena."

"I thought you would ask hesitantly." She said, raising up her sword.

Labara raised up her aduroblade against Savan-Nah's sword. The landscape was ready for the battle to begin at any moment. Tyrannus, steadily, turned his attention over to Jakah.

"Do it now."

"With pleasure."

Jakah pressed a series of buttons on his wrist, which caused his ship to hover in the air and begin firing at the Marvels, Savan-Nah, and Herena. Causing Tyrannus to send the rainshockers at them. Savan-Nah noticed the rainshockers and waved her arm.

"Marvels! Attack!"

The Marvels let out a yell as they ran for the rainshockers and the rainshockers toward them. Herena and Tyrannus clashed blades with one another as did Savan-Nah and Labara.

Jakah hovered up into the air with his jetpack, firing at the Marvels on the ground with his plasma-range. The howlsoldiers move with silence and stealth, making their way through the battlefield, taking down as many Marvels as they possibly could. Jakah continued firing at them from the air.

"They'll never know what hit them." He said.

A twirling sound is heard coming from behind Jakah. As he turned to see what it could be, he noticed it is a gold aduroblade, the blade swiped Jakah's jetpack, causing him to crash onto the ground. Tyrannus noticed and swiped his aduroblade against Herena with much more strength. He went in close and looked into her eyes.

"Where did you get the aduroblade from, woman?!"

"I didn't get one. It belongs to him."

"Him?!"

Tyrannus shoved Herena back against the temple's post and looked behind him, seeing the aduroblade in the hands of a man, dressed in armor with a brown and white tunic and cloak. Dressed as a Knight of the Covenant. Tyrannus stood and faced him.

"You are him." Tyrannus said boldly. "You are Jad Serkelrod. Five generations from Yabel Serkelrod. Son of Mehar Serkelrod."

"That I am." Jad said. "I'm wondering why you're here on Ellada, Viper Lord."

"The same could be asked of you, One of the Avior."

"Tell me, why are you here?"

"That is not the concern as this moment. Since you're here, I can finish what my master tried to do and that is defeat you."

"Sinth Zane didn't have the strength to take me down. What makes you believe you could?"

"Because I am not like my master and the Dekar is

stronger with me than it was with my master.”

Jad raised up his aduroblade, so did Tyrannus. Both were ready for their fight. One of the Dekar against One of the Avior.

“Let us see if your words speak truth or if they speak deception.”

Tyrannus raised up his adorable and approached Jad and the two clashed with their aduroblades, giving off the sound of a booming thunder.

IV
BATTLE OF OLYMPYA

Tyrannus and Jad continued clashing their aduroblades against one another. As they fight, the Marvels of the Universe battle it out against the rainshockers and howlsoldiers. Savan-Nah dueled with Labara as Herena approached the downed Jakah. He looked and saw her standing near him. He chose to let out a small laugh.

"This is unexpected." Jakah said.

"I noticed your weapon was aimed at me. I wasn't pleased." Herena said. "So, why don't you stand up and face me direct rather than behind your boss' back."

Jakah stood up and faced Herena. He tossed his plasma-range to the ground and smacked his fists in his hands.

"I'll face you. Hand to hand."

"So be it, mercenary scum."

Herena lunged toward Jakah with her fist, Jakah caught her fist and jumped over her, kicking her in the head. Herena's head bounced forward and Jakah landed on the ground and tackled her down. He held her down while he pummeled her in the face. Herena took the attacks and tossed Jakah off her with her strength. Jakah scoffed.

"You're stronger than I thought."

"Don't stop and talk now."

They continue their fight as Jad and Tyrannus's fight

could be heard throughout the battlefield. Loud booms emitting from countless impacts of the blades. In the midst of the battle, a man came from the mountains with blades of his own. The Marvels knew who he was and cheered at his appearance. The Viper Lords and Jakah were unaware as to who this mysterious stranger was. Jakah kicked Herena to the ground and approached the stranger. He wore a tunic from the waist down, strapped leather boots with metallic plating alongside two armguards similar to the boots. His eyes were yellow like Ellada's sun. He had little to no hair on his head and no beard.

"Who are you?"

"A warrior of the Dodekatheon. You're trespassing on their territory. And mine!"

The warrior lunged at Jakah, attacking and striking with his blades. Jakah flew into the air, knocking the warrior from him. The warrior landed on the ground and threw his blade, impacting with Jakah's jetpack, causing the hunter to crash. The Marvels saw this and praised.

"Cratos!" They yelled. "Cratos!"

Tyrannus kicked Jad in his left knee and elbowed him, staggering the Knight. Tyrannus held his blade higher and forward, rushing toward Jad. Jad flipped over Tyrannus, slashing the Viper Lord's cloak in half. Tyrannus ceased himself in his steps, reaching behind his back, feeling the heat from the burnt cloak. He turned around to see several pieces of it laying on the ground and in front of him by a few feet, Jad stood, twirling his aduroblade.

"You've proven yourself well." Tyrannus said. "A shame such good things must come to an end."

"That's where you're wrong. Things have only just begun."

While the two opposing forces stared one another down, the Marvels were defeating the shockers and Jakah was taken down by Cratos' might. His warrior skills proved too much for a venator such as Jakah. He was not dead, but down. The Marvels cheered their victory due to the assistance of Cratos and Jad. Although, Tyrannus was not done with the Knight just yet. He took the Sinthblade from its sheath and slashed Jad's chest, creating a deep wound. Jad fell to the ground, holding his chest in pain. He did not let out a single sound of agony as Tyrannus stood over him, smiling. Labara ran toward him, pleading they must reach Mount Oros.

"Take that mark as a sign of this battle. For the next time we meet, one of us will die."

The Viper Lords ran from the scene as the Marvels celebrated their victory. Olympya was protected by its own. Jad was helped up by Savan-Nah. Jakah silently returned to his ship, leaving the planet with a few rainshockers with him. While the Elladians took in their victory, Tyrannus and Labara were on their way to seek an audience with the Dodekatheon.

V

THE DODEKATHEON

Sinth Tyrannus and Sinth Labara walked far from the battlefield and reached Mount Oros, the sacred place of all Ellada. Tyrannus gazed up toward the top, which he could not see as it was shrouded by clouds. He pointed toward the top as Labara looked on.

"They're at the top." Tyrannus said. "That is where we must go."

"How will we get there?" Labara questioned, seeing as the mountain is very, very, very tall. "Do we take a ship?"

"We could. But, I prefer we go on foot. With the Dekar guiding us, I'm sure we'll get there faster than most."

Tyrannus and Labara made their move toward the top. Taking each step on foot. Duing their hike, they never grew tired or hungry. Sweat never poured from their skin and their breath was steady. The Dekar preserved them all the way to the top. Once upon the top, they found themselves standing in the center of what appeared to be a judgment room. The room was large and nearly forty stories in height. The walls decorated in gold and burnt brass, layered with lilies and vines. In the midst sat two cauldrons of fire.

"Mighty Gods of Oros!" Tyrannus yelled. "We have come

167

to have an audience!"

The room began to shift and in front of the cauldron opposite of the Viper Lords appeared twelve thrones. Upon those thrones sat the gods of Ellada. The gods of Oros themselves, known as the Dodekatheon. Tyrannus and Labara bowed before their presence, showing honor toward them in reverence of their power and authority over Ellada.

Sitting to the Viper Lords' left were as follows: *Hermaion*, Messenger of the Gods, Elladian God of Commerce, Thieves, Eloquence, and Streets. *Haphaistios*, Elladian God of Fire, Master Blacksmith and Craftsmen of the Gods. *Aphorodita*, Elladian Goddess of Love, Beauty, and Desire. *Areios*, Elladian God of War, Violence, and Bloodshed. *Artemas*, Elladian Goddess of Hunting, Virginity, Archery, Moon, and Animals.

Sitting to the Viper Lords' right were as follows: *Apellaios*, Elladian God of Light, Prophecy, Inspiration, Poetry, Music, and Art. *Athenai*, Elladian Goddess of Wisdom, War, Science, and Literature. *Damater*, Elladian Goddess of Fertility, Agriculture, Nature, and Seasons. *Posieidawon*, Elladian God of the Seas, Earthquakes, and Tidal Waves. *Hestva*, Elladian Goddess of Hearth, Domestication, and Family and *Hora-Uno*, Queen of the Elladian Gods and Goddess of Marriage and Family.

Lastly, sitting in the middle of the pantheon was *Emperor Dyeus*, the Elladian God of Thunder and the Sky, Ruler of Mount Oros. Tyrannus stood up and looked toward the gods of Oros. Their thrones and height were far beyond the Viper Lord's own. He looked at them further.

"I thought there were more of you."

"Two are elsewhere." Dyeus said with a commanding voice. "What brings the servants of The Fallen One to our mountain?"

"We come seeking an alliance."

"An alliance with non-worshipers?"

"This is for a greater cause." Tyrannus added. "We share a common enemy. The Knights of the Covenant. The servants of The High One."

"The Knights of The High One have never sought to take us out or to destroy our position. We do what we must. What we were placed to do."

"But, these are different times than before. More so than the Cavalier Civil War. These Knights aren't as forgiving and honorable as their ancestors. They're vicious. Whomever they seek to destroy, they do at a quickening pace. You will not see them coming."

Dyeus took in their words, sitting back in his throne as the other gods glared toward the Viper Lords. They could sense the Dekar upon them, searing out with great power. Dark power. Dyeus leaned in forward to the Viper Lords.

"If we aid you, what shall we be given in return?"

"As our Fallen One proclaims, you will receive a great portion of the universe and the sectors you can rule. You can gain more worshippers from across the stars and doing so, will put you and your pantheon atop the universe near our Fallen One."

"He speaks of more worshippers out there?" Hara-Uno asked.

"More servants to our cause will greatly make things better." Dyeus said. "Our work will be seen by all within the sectors. Showcasing our dominance across the stellarspace itself."

"What do you say, Emperor of Oros?" Tyrannus asked. "Will you come to terms from our Fallen One?"

"Your god is clever. But, manages a great strategy of dominance. We shall give it time and speak to your god face to face."

"Understood." Tyrannus said, bowing.

"As we should." Labara added.

"Now, leave us." Dyeus commanded. "Your god will deliver the response to you when it's time."

The Viper Lords left Mount Oros and Ellada, returning to Moraltis with what was left of their army. Sometime later, during a meditation process with Tyrannus and Labara, they were granted an utterance in the Dekar, signaling the agreement between the Dodekatheon and the Fallen One was in place. Settled in stone across the walls of the Moraltian Castle as well upon the base of Mount Oros.

"It is settled." Tyrannus said.

"Yes." Labara replied. "Our higher learning has begun."

VI
THE COMING HEIRS
349 YEARS DURING THE BATTLE OF CAELUM

Fifty-one years after the Battle of Olympya, the Viper Lords trained and mediated deeper into the Dekar. Many things changed across the sectors as the alliance between the Viper Lords and the Dodekatheon was now known across many nations. The Magus Court later came to terms of an agreement between Ordow and Moraltis.

Labara was in labor and she gave birth to her and Tyrannus' first child. A son. The child was named Cain and proclaimed to become a future Viper Lord. Upon his birth, the Dekar was infused within the infant as his eyes were the colors of a red sky, streaking with lightning. The priests entered the chambers after the birth and praised the child. After the priests gave out their praise, the Supreme Cardinal entered the chamber and gazed upon the son. He bowed and nodded his head.

"The lineage of the Dekar will continue with this one. For I sense the power already surging in him. Lords Tyrannus and Labara, guide him well. Teach him ours ways as you were taught in your youths. Make him love the Fallen One with all his heart. Always let the Dekar guide his footsteps as it has and is guiding yours."

The Cardinal began speaking in Moraltian tongues over him. Cain was destined to become a powerful Viper Lord.

Elsewhere, on the planet of Erets-Alpha in the country lands near the city of Coolts, there was a woman giving birth at approximately the same exact time as Labara. This woman was Desta Serkelrod, the wife of Laban Serkelrod, son of Jad. Their child was a son as well and he was called Aweran Serkelrod. Desta smiled as she placed her eyes upon him, proclaiming he is the "beginning restoration". Aweran was destined to become one of the Knights of the Covenant as were his fathers who came before.

VII
THE CONJUNCTION
335 YEARS DURING THE BATTLE OF CAELUM

Tyrannus and Labara traveled to Sinstor to meet with Pharao Khopra-Ahr, the ruler of the Late Period Dynasty of Sinstor. The Late Period came into place after the death of Amran-Em-Of and fall of his New Kingdom. The Viper Lords arrived in Misriaym and entered the palace. They stood before the Pharao in the throne room and showed obeisance toward him. All in honor.

"It is good to see great allies once more." Khopra said.

"We've come to you after we heard word of assistance." Tyrannus said.

"Very well. Then, you know about the Emerald Cavaliers and their interference in Sinstor's growth."

"We've heard the Knights are also involved." Labara said. "What have they done so far?"

"They're aiding the Cavaliers against us. Things aren't as they were during the War of Helio. However, this is a new age and things cannot be ruled the same. So, I ask of you to assist me in countering the attacks of this Cavaliers and the Knights, whom you know much of."

Tyrannus nodded.

"We will aid you, Pharao. For in fact, we are already allies as were the fathers before our time."

"Those who knew what they could achieve." Khopra

added. "Yes, we already are."

The Viper Lords left the Pharao's presence and with this alliance, the Pharao commanded his scribes to write down the names of Tyrannus and Labara upon the walls of the throne room, engraving them within the other hieroglyphics across the walls.

VIII
AVIOR VS. DEKAR
325 YEARS DURING THE BATTLE OF CAELUM

Ten years later, Tyrannus and Labara sat in the throne room of the Moraltian Castle, mediating into the Dekar. Over those ten years, the Viper Order increased in strength and power. In the middle of their mediation, they were contacted by their Emperor. He appeared in a dark shrouded mist in their sight. They saw him and bowed.

"We weren't aware of your visitation, master." Tyrannus said. "What is your command?"

"He two of you have grown profoundly in the Dekar. The Viper Order is recognized as a tremendous superpower across the sectors. However, there is another power which rivals ours. The Avior. It is growing as well. Creating a rift through the cosmos. You know what must be done. Go to Helio and eliminate the Knights of the Covenant. Bury the Avior's power for all eternity!"

"We will do as you have spoken." Tyrannus said.

"It will be done, master." Labara added. "We shall not fail."

"I know you won't. Now go."

The mist evaporated as the Lords stood tall. They equipped themselves and the rainshockers. Without haste, they traveled to Helio. Making their landing in the wilderness outside of the city of Tropolton. They knew how to manipulate the radars of the planet to avoid capture. The rainshockers ran out with ranges in hands the Lords exit the ship last. They made their way toward the city and before they could reach it, an aduroblade appeared from the trees, slashing several rainshockers in half. The blade twirled and returned to its user who walked out from the bushes.

"I see." Tyrannus said.

Standing before them was a Knight of the Covenant. Dressed in the same garb as those before. The energy of the blade glowed a dark blue. He stood firm before Tyrannus and Labara.

"You're trespassing."

"And who might you be?" Labara asked.

"I am Laban, son of Jad Serkelrod."

Tyrannus stepped further, pulling out his aduroblade.

"A Serkelrod?! Where is your father?"

"On Knight duty. What's your purpose here, Moraltian?"

"Tell me this, before I kill you, how old are you?"

"How old are you?"

"I'm older than your father. Now you."

"Fifty-five years during this Battle of Caelum."

"Ah." Tyrannus nodded. "Good prime age for a warrior. Howbeit that this day is your last."

"Just get ready to fight." Laban raised his blade.

"Fair enough."

Tyrannus and Laban clashed their blades against each other. The two battled it our within the wilderness as Labara took the remaining rainshockers and headed toward the city. Laban fought with striking blows as Tyrannus moved quickly, swiping his aduroblade toward Laban's knees. Laban raised his hands, using the Avior to blow back the Viper Lord. Tyrannus was impressed at his skills.

"You know how to use your true power."

"When it's necessary."

"What is more necessary than preserving your life!"

Tyrannus forcefully caused a tree to come crashing down as Laban jumped out of its way and collided once more with Tyrannus, who laughed during the fight. Laban shoved Tyrannus and swiped the blade against the Viper Lord's chest, cutting the armor. Tyrannus nodded with a smirk.

"Oh good." Tyrannus scoffed.

He grabbed Laban and head-butted the Knight. Laban stood up from the blow and they continued clashing the blades. Through the clashes, the blades sparked against one another as the air was being absorbed by them. Laban was losing his breath.

"Can't you count on your Avior to aid you?!"

"Do not mock the power of The High One."

"I'll mock until I'm dead."

"Then, prepare to fall as did your Fallen One!"

Laban pushed back, regaining his breath as he took steps to avoid Tyrannus' incoming attacks. Laban turned, kicking Tyrannus to the ground. He moved and stood over the Viper Lord with his blade over his throat.

"You've lost here."

"Haven't they taught you anything?"

Labara appeared from behind Laban, swiping him in his back with her own aduroblade as Tyrannus shoved him back and rushed him with the Sinthblade, impaling him in the chest. Laban fell to the ground as the Viper Lords stood over him.

"I truly hope your Knights aren't as ceasing as you."

"My bretheren will avenge me as will my son."

"Your son?" Tyrannus asked. "Well, I hope to meet your son. For if I do, he'll soon be joining you in the higher realm."

Laban was dead as the Viper Lords made their way toward

Tropolton.

IX
THE GREAT PURGE

The rainshockers invaded the city of Tropolton as the Knights of the Covenant were caught off guard due to their ongoing conflicts with the Magus Court and concerns surrounding the power of the Dekar across the sectors. Rainshockers shot down and killed anyone who came into their sights. From the Temple of the Avior rushed out the Knights. Those Knights were Nidd Sycl-Derdr, Giphbel Tykm, and Mossh El-Jiad, All armed with aduroblades as they quickly rid of the rainshockers, leaving Tyrannus and Labara last. The three Knights made their moves against the Viper Lords, but they were too inexperienced against Those of the Dekar. They did however fight with great strength and honor, but their focus was scattered in between, saving the people, fighting the Viper Lords, and evacuating the city itself.

Afterwards, walked out four more Knights. They were led by Amzi Grake. He saw Tyrannus and Labara and went to fight against them. Amzi and Tyrannus fought each other as more rainshockers arrived, giving room for the other Knights to take them out. Labara stood back as she did not want to fight three Knights on her own, as they would've surely taken her out quickly. Amzi was strong naturally and spiritually as the Avior was overtaking the Dekar in the battle and Tyrannus grew tired. Amzi knocked both the aduroblade and

Sinthblade from Tyrannus' grasp and decapitated the Viper Lord. Labara witnessed his head fall from his body and she let out a purging scream of agony. To the point where she took out her own aduroblade and impaled herself. She fell to the ground as the Knights watched her crawl toward her husband as she died by his side.

The city was in flames and more rainshockers were arriving as was more Moraltian enforcements.

"What shall we do?" A Knight said to Amzi.

"We must leave. Return another day."

Amzi led the remaining Knights of the Covenant as they fled into the wilderness of Helio.

THE ANCIENT KNIGHTS OF ELYON

325 BOC
325 YEARS DURING THE *BATTLE OF CAELUM*

I
THE LAST ONES

"Before the world you've known, there existed an age of extraordinary proportions." - The High One

Upon the treachery and defeat of the Abhdi against the Viper Order, the remaining Knights of the Ancient Covenant fled into the wilderness and hid from the Viper Order and their massive army of Rainshockers. There were four Knights that escaped from the hands of the Viper Order and their leader, Sinth Tyrannus and his wife, Sinth Labara. Tyrannus and Labara fell in battle to the Abhdi Knights. But, it wasn't enough to save the Abhdi Knights themselves. Now, the Viper Order has placed two new Viper Lords in the places of Tyrannus and Labara. Sinth Cain and his wife, Sinth Kara. Their first task is to hunt down the remaining Knights and exterminate them from existence along with their beliefs and sovereign ideals. The four Knights that escaped were Orvan Shackleford, Novad Tengu, Ebed El-Ezer, and their leading Abhdi Master, Amzi Grake.

Walking through the wilderness of their home planet called Helio, a planet that was the homeland of the Old Covenant, a land ruled by sovereignty and peace before it was sacked and taken over by the Viper Lords eons after eons, Amzi leads the remaining Knights through the wilderness, moving quietly as they can to avoid any possible disturbance that could give away their signal to the roaming rainshockers lurking around the forest. Their robes show the signs of war, ripped in parts and burned in others. Blood stained across their loose-fitting pants and chest.

"Master, what is our plan exactly?" Orvan said. "We're nearly exhausted and we don't know if we can move much longer like this."

"Knight Orvan, keep your worrisome words to yourself." Amzi said. "Do not speak of them in such a manner. For what you shall speak will become your reality."

"What of the refugee base out here?" Novad said. "Perhaps we should proceed there to find any aid in our mission."

"You are correct, Knight Novad. Come, let us seek out the refugee base. That way we can regain the strength we've lost in this treacherous battle."

They move on through the wilderness. Ebed pulled Amzi to the side and looked around at the trees.

"Master, the Viper Order will not stop until they've killed all of us."

"I understand that. But, we cannot back down from a fight against them if they happen to come across our pathway."

"They killed three of our brothers in arms."

"I know. I was there when they crossed over. I witnessed it all." Amzi said. "Ebed, you must listen to me, we were promised to live through such circumstances like this one. In time, we will overcome them like our ancient ancestors have done."

Amzi pats Ebed on his right shoulder and smiled. Ebed nodded to Amzi.

"Come on, let's get to that base."

Walking for a few miles through the wilderness, the Knights find themselves looking out toward a small base surrounded by evacuees from Tropolton, the capital city of Helio. They walked toward the base as the people turned and looked upon them. Spotting their robes and their presence, they know they're Abhdi Knights and immediately the people run toward them, begging to know of their cities' current circumstance.

"People of Tropolton, please calm yourself and we will explain all that we know of your city."

"What of our city?"" A refugee said. "What about our families out there?!"

"What we do know is the city has been sacked by the Viper Order." Amzi said. "But, some of our fellow Knights managed to slay Sinth Tyrannus and his wife took her own life afterwards out of fear of imprisonment."

"When can we go back?" Another refugee said. "When can we return to our homes?"

"We do not know if you'll ever return to your homes."

The people gasped in fear and dread of never seeing their homes again. Amzi stood before them and raised his hand. Calming and relaxing them from their fears.

"We will restore Tropolton in time and you'll have your city back and your planet well protected."

"How can you be so sure of that, Knight of Abhdi?" One refugee said. "How can we trust your words?"

"Trust not my words, but the actions that will ensure its protection."

The people stood quiet as Amzi and the Knights continued to walk toward the main section of the base. They sat underneath a tent until nightfall. While sitting, they ate and drank while discussing their next phase of action.

"We'll need some assistance." Amzi said.

"We surely do, Master." Ebed said. "But, I'm not so sure we'll find them here."

"We need younger assistance. Younger warriors that will one day take our place as Knights of Abhdi and bring them into becoming Those of the Avior."

"Are you sure its appropriate that we do such a task now?" Orvad said. "When could we find them?"

"Not sure at the moment." Amzi said. "But, it will come up when the time is appointed."

After several hours when the people took themselves to sleep and the Knights took some time to rest up, a group of rainshockers slowly made their way into the base wearing their dark gray and white clad armor, they slowly raised up their plasma-ranges and aimed them toward the people sleeping. The commanding rainshocker raised up his hand and moved it down.

"Take the shots!" The Rainshocker Commander said."

The rainshockers started firing at the people who woken up in an instantly screaming in fear. The Knights were also awake and took notice at the rainshockers. They stood up and counted them.

"There's ten of them, Master." Novad said. "What shall we do about them?"

"Eliminate as many as you possibly can." Amzi said. "We're here to protect the people."

The Knights walked out of their tent and pulled out their main choice of weapon from their sides, out of their sheaths, the aduroblade. A weapon similar to a sword, made of minerals from the stars and coated with a plasma energy. Amzi's aduroblade glows blue, Ebed's glows green, Novad's glows yellow, and Orvan's glows orange. They run out into the open and combat the rainshockers, using their aduroblades to block the shots from the rainshockers' plasma-ranges. They ram toward the shockers, swiping off their limbs with the aduroblades and killing them with blows to the abdomen and back. Amzi turned and looked out into the forest, seeing more rain shockers coming their way. He faces the Knights, waving at them to exit the base.

"We have to leave!" Amzi said. "More are coming."

"Master." Ebed said.

The Knights fled the base as about a dozen more rainshockers stormed through the base, killing whomever remained. In the woods, the Knights ran as fast as they possibly could with as little rest they've received. They took a brief moment to catch their breaths as the sounds of the plasma-ranges were fading away in the distance.

"What are we to do now, Master?" Novad said.

"Brothers, it seems that in order to find our new recruits, we'll have to leave Helio and leave here fast."

"Where are we to go?" Orvan said.

"We'll go to Erets-Alpha. I am certain we'll find our young members there. Plus, the planet has a wall that forbids the Viper Order from entering their atmosphere."

"We'll need a ship, Master." Ebed said.

"I know. We'll have to make a quiet return to Tropolton and reclaim our ship."

"Its too dangerous, Master." Orvan said.

"Its our only option as of this moment." Amzi said. "We will return to Tropolton by nightfall, reclaim our ship and leave this planet for Erets-Alpha."

"We understand your words, Master." Ebed said.

Amzi nodded as he and the Knights made their way back toward Tropolton while moving quietly from the surrounding armies of rainshockers.

II
PREPARE THYSELF

Returning to Tropolton through the wilderness, avoiding the rain shockers that are swarming through the land, Amzi leads the Knights back to the now desolate city and its decimated temple. The Knights take a look around their surroundings, hearing the sounds of the rainshockers' machines walking through the woods, stomping and crushing downed branches, moving through the bushes.

"They brought the Raubtiers with them." Orvad said.

"They were prepared for the battle that they sought." Amzi said. "We have to keep moving. Make our way toward the temple."

Making their move through the woods, a land-veho passes them by, rode by one of the rainshockers. A land-veho is a hovering vehicle similar to a motorcycle without its wheels.

"They have the vehoes with them too." Novad said. "They were prepared."

"They surely were." Amzi said. "Let's keep moving."

The land-vehoes come flying past them through the woods as they made their way through.

On the planet called Moraltis, the home world of the

Viper Order, Sinth Cain and Sinth Kara, dressed in their hooded black, scarlet, and red cloaks and armored plated uniforms, sit on their thrones within the Moraltan Castle surrounded by rainshockers and cloaked advisers. Within the throne room, two rainshockers opened the doors, allowing a woman to enter. The woman walked in wearing hunting gear and equipped with a weapon of her own to her side, resembling a bullwhip. She approached Sinth Cain and Sinth Kara.

"Dos Ar-Suyaza." Sinth Kara said.

"Masters." She said.

She kneeled before them at their presence. Showing respect and honor towards her new Viper Lords. Sinth Cain nodded and lifted his hand up toward her. She raised up her head and faced him.

"Rise up, huntress." Sinth Cain said.

"I heard you called to require my assistance in a certain matter."

"We need your assistance on an urgent matter."

"Whatever my masters commands of."

"Good." Sinth Kara said. "Because it requires you to hunt down the remaining Knights of the Old Covenant."

"The Knights? I thought they were all but dead. Sinth Tyrannus and Sinth Labara insured us that he would've killed them all."

"But he didn't, did he?" Sinth Cain said. "Now, the task is in the hands of myself and my wife. We will complete the mission that the previous Lord failed to do."

"Where were they last sighted, masters?"

"On their home world of Helio." Sinth Cain said. "Tropolton is their precious city. They're fully armed with their blades."

Dos nodded in understanding. She looked back at the

rain shockers standing by the door.

"If I may ask humbly, masters. I will need a small army of my own to back me up in this bounty of yours."

"Sure." Sinth Kara said. "Take as many shockers as you please. Acquire the resources you will need at completing this task."

"When you make your move onto them. After you've killed them all, bring back their aduroblades as a remnant of their deaths."

"I will do so, masters."

Dos nodded as she left the throne room. Sinth Kara turned to Sinth Cain, smiling at him.

"Soon, my love, we will make a full end of those Ancient Knights and their foolish belief in the *Avior*."

"Do not underestimate the power of the *Avior* or the one who controls it." Sinth Cain said. "It has the power to wipe us all out if its pleased. There's a reason it is known as the adversary to the *Dekar*."

Amzi and the Knights have made it through the woods and into the city of Tropolton. Amzi looks at the city streets, seeing them occupied with rainshockers. Armed with their plasma-ranges and searching every building around them.

"We're gonna have to make a stealth way towards the temple." Amzi said. "Otherwise, we'll end up in a firestorm with them and our blades."

"So, how do we do this, master?" Orvad said.

"Follow my lead and we'll make a straightway towards the temple, gather our gear and get off of this planet."

"As you say." Novad said.

The Knights moved slowly and quietly through the streets. Hiding from the rainshockers on the roads nearby.

Moving as fast as they can through the street. They approach the temple steps and open its doors. Making their way inside, they see the damage that was left behind as well as the deceased corpses of their fallen brethren and Sinth Tyrannus and Sinth Labara. Amzi kneeled down at the bodies of his brethren and hung his head before them.

"Farewell, brothers." Amzi said. "We'll see you in the Next Life."

"What of their bodies, master?" Ebed said. "Shouldn't we bury them?"

"Yeah. We should."

The Knights had taken the time to bury the fallen in a small garden nearby the temple. Amzi grabbed the aduroblades of the fallen brethren and placed them in a vault within the walls of the temple, surrounded by other aduroblades and weapons from previous Knights of the Old Covenant. The Knights gathered the equipment they needed and proceed towards the ship called Helio Sor. A circular ship with a fin atop and two side that looked like wings.

"Ready to leave this place?" Amzi said.

"Ready we are."

They entered the ship and Amzi takes lead. Turning on the ship, its engine roars and gets the attention of the rainshockers, who make their way towards the temple entrance. Orvad looked out of the ship's window, seeing them coming.

"Rainshockers are coming, master."

"Give them a quick fight while the ship prepares herself for liftoff."

Orvad, Novad, and Ebed run down from the ship and begin fighting the rainshockers with their aduroblades as Amzi prepares the ship. Swiping the rain shockers with the blades. The ship roars, signaling its ready for takeoff.

"Come on!" Ebed said. "We have to leave now!"

The Knights run toward the ship, deflecting the firing shots from the rainshockers' plasma-ranges. They jump into the ship as it lifts itself up and bursts through the temple walls and flies into the air, vanishing into thin air with hyper speed. The rain shockers look above, no longer seeing the ship.

"Make sure our outer fleets have their eyes on sight for them." The leading rainshocker said to his group. "We cannot have them running loose out there."

III
A YOUNG ABHDI

The Knights arrive on the planet of Erets-Alpha. Flying through the air above its primary city of Coolts. The residents look up towards the ship and point. Astonished to see a ship of such valor and detail. The ship flew past the city, near the rural grounds in the outskirts of Coolts.

"Best we make a landing out here rather than near the city." Amzi said. "The crowd could bring us some trouble."

Amzi landed the ship in the middle of the country-like fields away from the city of Coolts. Once they exited the ship, Amzi locked it down and camouflaged the ship into the appearance of being invisible from prying eyes across the country fields. While they walked away and headed toward the nearest home for refugee, Amzi noticed a young man wandering in the woods nearby. The young man dressed in boots, loose-fitting pants, and a medieval style light tan tunic. His short cut black hair stood out from his uniform.

"Do you sense that power, Knights?" Amzi said.

"I sense it." Orvad said. "Where's it coming from?"

Amzi pointed toward the young man in the woods, cutting down bushes with a sword. Amzi stared at him and noticed his techniques with the sword. He could sense the young man had the potential to become one of the Knights of the Covenant or one of the Viper Lords.

"What's your plan with him, Master?" Novad said.

"Remember when I once said we'll need some assistance on our mission in defeating the Viper Order?"

"We do remember your words."

"That young man is the first step in accomplishing that task."

Amzi walked past the knights toward the woods to greet the young man. The Knights followed him as they came closer toward the woods and the young man. The young man chopped down a small tree and as it fell, he could see Amzi and the Knights approaching him. He stared at them with curiosity, he recognized their uniforms, their cloaks, and their aduroblades on their sides.

"It's them." The young man said.

Amzi and the Knights approach him as the tree fell and they could see the interest in the young man's eyes as he stared at them. Novad looks at the other Knights and turned toward Amzi.

"I think he knows who we are."

"That makes our meet and greet better than what could've happened if he didn't."

Amzi walked toward the young man and extended his hand. The young man shook his hand with a glinting smile coming from his face.

"Why do you smile, young one?" Amzi said.

"I recognize who you are." Aweran answered.

"Do tell."

"You're The Ancient Knights of Elyon. The Knights of the Old Covenant as some would call you."

"So, you know of us." Amzi said. "You know what our mission is in this life and you know what we strive for."

"I've done my study on your mission and what you desire to achieve."

"Is there a place nearby that we could rest at for a

moment?”

"You can come to my home. There's enough room for you all.”

"Splendid. Lead the way, young one.”

The young man led Amzi and the Knights to his home out in the rural lands. Once they approach the home, the young man opened the door and allowed them to enter, which he entered last and shut the door.

"Do any of you require water or food?”

"Water would be well." Amzi said. "So, young one what is your name?”

"My name's Aweran Serkelrod. Named after my great-great grandfather, Judios Aweran Serkelrod.”

"I know of him. He was a Knight as well. An Abhdi Knight who fought during the Rise of the Supremacy.”

"So I've heard he did. Shame I never had the chance to meet him.”

"Someday you will.”

Aweran brought the Knights some cups of water, which they drank without hesitation. Aweran noticed the cuts and stains of blood on the Knights' uniforms and cloaks.

"If you don't mind me asking, it appears you guys went through some kind of battle before coming here.”

"Our home planet of Helio was attacked by the Viper Order and they sacked our city of Tropolton with their armies of rainshockers. We Knights did our best effort to fight for our city, but it was not enough and we lost three of our brothers in the process.”

"I'm sorry to hear that.”

Amzi placed his cup onto the table and set an interest into what Aweran knows through his researching.

"Tell me, young one, what do you know about the Knights of the Covenant and the Viper Order?”

"I know that you've fought each other for thousands of years and continue to battle this day. I also am aware that the both of you have the ability to use the *Avior* and *Dekar* to your advantages in battle."

"You know of the Avior and the Dekar?" Novad said. "How much have you learned from them?"

"I have learned only what I have read. I take it that you Knights can harness the power of the Avior?"

"We surely can and you can too."

Aweran paused for a moment, slightly took a swallow and shook his head.

"I wouldn't know that to be a possibility." Aweran said. "I'm not a knight like you men."

"Tell me this, Aweran, if you were given the opportunity to leave your home and travel with us, we would train you, make you a Knight of the Covenant. An Abhdi Knight. You could help save souls from the Viper Order and bring peace across the universe. Would you turn down such an offer?"

"I wouldn't know what to say if it were to come up."

Amzi nodded. "Aweran, it has come up and I am giving you that opportunity right this moment. By morning, you can come with us and save souls, become a Knight of the Covenant, bring peace to the universe or you can decline such an offer and remain here at your home. An average living where life and death flow through the lands like the winds of the air flow through the trees.

"I wouldn't know what to truly say."

"You have until the sun rises the morrow." Amzi said. "Take your time to meditate on it, your life requires of it."

Amzi and the Knights went into the others rooms of the home and stayed their to rest the entire day. Before the sunset, Aweran gathered the cut down bushes and small trees and carried them near his home where he would used them for firewood. While gathering the wood, he could hear a snarl coming from within the dark woods. Aweran looked around for his sword, but it was in the house, laying near the door.

"Dammit." Aweran said.

From the woods jumped out above Aweran an Oxow, a four-legged beast of great strength, which its hide shined a light brown from the downed sun and the rising moon. The oxow roared at Aweran as it tackled him down to the ground and stood atop him, trying to impale at his neck with its horns. Aweran held the beast above him with his strength and yelled for help.

From the home ran out Amzi, who eyes caught the beast and he pulled out his aduroblade. Aweran threw the oxow off of him and stood up to the beast. He turned around seeing Amzi.

"Aweran, use this!" Amzi said, tossing his aduroblade to Aweran.

Aweran caught the aduroblade and once it was grasped the blade became coated in the blue aura of energy that gave it its power. The oxow lunged at Aweran, its horns straight out, and with one swipe of the aduroblade, the oxow was killed and its body fell to the ground, cut in half as if it was butter to a heated knife.

"Not bad, young one." Amzi said. "Good things it was not an Daseur."

The other Knights walked out of the home to see Amzi and Aweran standing next to the dead oxow. They walked toward them in the field near the woods where they could see Aweran holding Amzi's aduroblade in his hands.

"Why is he holding your aduroblade, Master?" Orvad said. "He's not supposed to use your blade."

"He had no weapon on him when the beast attacked."

Amzi said. "The only option was to hand him my aduroblade and through that he survived the attack and killed the beast."

Amzi looked at Aweran with the aduroblade in his hands. He nodded with a grin on his face.

"He also showed he can wield an aduroblade without any problems what so ever."

Aweran handed the aduroblade back to Amzi, who returned it to his side. Aweran looked at the dead beast and gave a circular look around the lands. From the homes around him to the woods behind him. He turned to Amzi after gazing around the land.

"What is it, young one?" Amzi said.

"You know, I've always wondered what my life should be. The path that is. When I held your aduroblade, I felt a presence. Similar to that of my father and his father before him. I should become a Knight like the forefathers of old."

"Does that mean you have answered the opportunity?"

"It has. I'm coming along with you."

Amzi smiled and hugged Aweran with great energy.

"Splendid! You have much to learn, young one."

Amzi and Aweran returned to the home with the Knights following them. They took the dead body of the oxow and burned it as an offering to The High One, to watch over them and give them more power through the use of the *Avior*. The smoke of the offering arose into the air, touching the dusk sky.

Miles away from Erets-Alpha, Dos Ar-Suyaza and her small army of rainshockers landed on Helio and entered the city of Tropolton. She commanded the rainshockers to search the temple for any sign of the escaped Knights. Meanwhile, she walked around the place and could sense the aura of the former Viper Lords.

"So, this is where you both passed on." Dos said. "A

place that wasn't a part of your beliefs nor your ambitions."

She could see the stains of their blood on the golden floors of the temple. She rubbed them with an handkerchief and placed it into her pants pocket. From the temple doors came the rainshockers.

"What have you found?"

"Nothing." A rainshocker said. "No sign of the Knights were found around here."

"Are you sure of that?"

"We are positive. They had to have escaped and left the planet."

Dos nodded and walked past the rainshockers toward the outside. Her anger could been seen on her face and felt in the hearts of the rainshockers.

"Looks like we have more lands to search."

IV
AREA 6776

The following morning on Erets-Alpha in the rural area, Aweran prepared his gear as he walked with the Knights toward their ship, which was parked in the distance from Aweran's home. As they entered the ship, Aweran approached Amzi.

"So, may I ask where are we headed?"

"We will need more young recruits to aid us in this quest. We're going to pay 6776 a visit."

"Area 6776?" Aweran said. "Isn't that a infamous prison planet for bounty hunters and mercenaries?"

"It is." Orvad said." "A place where many do not return to their natural state."

"We need a man there. His cunning ability can prove to be of great use and would bring confusion upon the Viper Order."

"How will we know who to look for, Master?" Novad said.

"It's simple, we'll walk in and ask for his name."

"You know his name already, Master?" Orvad said.

"I do. I know him as well. We have a history with one another that contains a smuggling act he did back in Tropolton. This will be him paying me back for saving his life the last time we met."

"Is he a nice guy?" Aweran said.

"He's a cynical one. Sarcasm is his second language."

Amzi approached the pilot seat and prepares the ship for takeoff. The Knights and Aweran buckle up in their seats, sitting across from each other in rows as the ship slowly hovers and takes off into the air. Aweran looked through the window, seeing his home, possibly for the last time as he looked toward the sky, seeing the blue with the clouds as it evaporated away into a deep darkness where only the dots of the stars could be seen.

Another ship flew through the stellarspace, within the ship walked Dos Ar-Suyaza as she spoke with Sinth Cain through a red hologram projector. She had told him there were no signs of the Knights back on Helio in Tropolton.

"They will not be far, huntress." Sinth Cain said. "I suggest you keep looking and search the place where they would last be seen by prying eyes."

"I will do so, master."

"Make your Viper Lords proud, huntress. Show the Viper Order that you are worthy of your place with us."

"I will."

Sinth Cain's hologram disappeared as Dos walked toward the piloting rainshockers. She stood behind them, gazing out into the abyss of space. Seeing nothing but the stars and distant planets.

"Make way for 6776." Dos said.

"Why would we need to go there." The pilot said. "What would even make it believable to find the Ancient Knights there?"

"Trust me. We make way for Area 6776."

"Yes ma'am." The second pilot said. "On route to

Sector 6776. One way."

The Helio Sor makes its way closer to Area 6776 to where Aweran and the Knights are able to see the prison planet in the distance from the ship. Amzi pilots the ship toward the planet. Orvad sat next to Aweran to ask him questions concerning the task.

"If you could choose between the Avior or the Dekar, which would you prefer?"

"How can I answer a question like that?"

"It's a question you answer from the mind. The heart will automatically submit to the Dekar because its comfortable and easier. The Avior takes much work to gain and to keep. I hope for your sake, young one, you gain the Avior and will be able to stand on the frontlines of war with us."

"Time will only give us that answer, Knight Orvad."

"I am well certain of that."

After about twenty minutes, Amzi speaks to Aweran and the Knights that the ship is about to land on Area 6776. The Knights prepare themselves and place their audroblades to their sides.

Aweran looked around and possessed no weapon of his own. Reaching to his sides.

"Master Amzi, I have no weapon of my own."

"You'll have a weapon of your own eventually." Amzi said. "Trust me."

Amzi flies the ship through the lines of the prison planet and prepares to land in the rugged lands near the entrance to the prison. Upon landing, Aweran and the Knights exited the ship and approach the entrance doors and were stopped by 6776 patrolmen.

"What is your business here, gentlemen?"

"We are here to pick up a prisoner." Amzi said. "He is needed of great importance to a major cause."

"Is that all your business requires here?"

"That is our business here. We'll pick him up and we'll be gone."

The patrolmen moved to the size, giving them entrance into the prison. Amzi nodded as they walked through the entrance doors and into the prison. Within the prison structure, they noticed cells of a vast number, ranging from floors from where they stood to floors deep beneath the planet grounds.

"Do you know which floor he is on, master?" Orvad said.

"I do not know." Amzi said. "I will ask the lady at the counter there. She will tell us."

Amzi approached the counter and the lady startled when she looked up toward him. He could sense that she knew he was an Abhdi Knight of the Covenant. He raised his hand up. Open. Commanding her to stay silent in order to avoid patrolmen near the counter. She nodded.

"Do not say a word, my lady. We present to you no harm."

"May I ask why you're here?"

"We're here to pick up a prisoner."

"The name please?"

"Evad Nod."

"The smuggler?" The receptionist said bluntly.

"Yes, my lady."

"Will his weapons be picked up in this matter?"

"Most certainty." Amzi said. "Where he's going, he will need them."

The woman looked onto the computer monitor on her

desk. She handed Amzi a card, which he took and looked at it, seeing it marked with numbers and codes.

"Evad Nod is placed on the third floor beneath us. You can go down there and pick him up yourselves if you like."

"We will do so. Thank you for your assistance, my lady."

Amzi lead Aweran and the Knights down to the elevator. They entered and Amzi placed the card within the slider and typed in the floor number. The elevator doors closed as they slowly went down to the third floor.

"Do you feel something going on around here, Master?" Aweran said.

"There are many things that take place here, Aweran. Things that would make the heart of a man or woman cold and cruel."

They make their stop on the third floor and the elevator doors opened, revealing the floor covered with patrolmen walking down the corridors. Amzi looked around.

"Which way do we proceed?" Orvad said.

"Follow me and we'll be just fine."

They walked out of the elevator and down the first corridor, where Amzi looked at the card, which contained the number of the corridor and cell block where Evad was kept. While they walked down the hall, they passed by a woman. Her aura connected with Aweran, who stopped and stared at her. She looked at him and directed her eyes toward the cell and to Amzi. Aweran nodded and stopped Amzi.

"Master, she is being kept her on wrong charges."

"What makes you say that, Aweran?"

"Her aura, I can sense it. She's been wrongly placed here."

"Let me ask her."

Amzi stepped back and faced the woman in the cell.

She looked at him with hope in her eyes. Amzi could also sense her aura coming through the cell. He nodded with a smile on his face. He turned to the Knights.

"We have another one, Knights."

"How are we to get her out of here, master?" Ebed said.

"We'll have to get Evad out first. We'll come back for her once Evad is out of the cell. Then we'll make our leave."

They continued walking down the corridor until they stopped at the cell where Evad was kept. Amzi stood in front of the cell, seeing Evad, sitting down with his head turned toward the wall. Amzi tapped on the cell bars to get his attention. Evad waved his hand at him.

"Go away, jack off. I do not want to be bothered by you totalitarian idiots."

"We're not totalitarian as you might know, Mr. Nod." Amzi said. "Turn yourself around to the cell bars and see."

Evad turned to the cell door, seeing Amzi he sood up and approached the cell bars with a smile on his face.

"Great to see you, Amzi."

"Like old times you would say."

"In a matter of speaking." Evad said. "Except this time, you're not on the other side of the cell with me."

"I've changed my ways, old friend."

"You sure have. Why have you come to visit me?"

"I'm here to give you your release."

"My release?"

"I need your assistance in an urgent matter taking place across the universe. Your skills are heavily needed."

"Fair enough. Just get me out of here so I can get my shit back."

"I can tell they have your range?"

"They surely do. They keep it locked in with these other stooges' gear. Mashed around, but I'll know it when I see it. My initials are carved on the handle.”

Amzi nodded sarcastically, “Interesting.”

Amzi placed the card into the cell door’s slider and it unlocked the cell, releasing Evad, who moved out of the cell quickly and looked around the corridor.

“Where are the patrolmen?”

“Walking about their business. No need to worry of them.”

“Are you sure about that?”

“I am. Right now we need to get someone else out of this place.”

“What someone else?”

“A woman wrongly placed here.”

“Now that is something of a discussion. Did you know there are more women imprisoned in this place than men.”

“I can speculate as to why.”

“I’m sure you can. You know a lot about the life we all live in.”

“I don’t know a lot, Evad. I know enough to continue living in the right place of mind.”

They walked down the corridor, returning to the woman’s cell. When Amzi stood in front of the cell bars, the woman’s face began to glow with joy. Amzi could sense her happiness rising from within her.

“Don’t you worry, young lady.” Amzi said. “We’re getting you out of here too.”

“Isn’t that card only designed to release Evad from his cell, master?” Orvad said.

“It is programmed that way.” Amzi said. “Though, I made some minor changes to it when she handed it to me.”

“What kind of changes?” Evad said. “I’m intrigued to know.”

“I’ll tell you another time. You might end up here

again you know.”

“Real funny of you, old friend.”

Amzi slid the card into the slider and opened the cell doors for the young lady, who ran out and hugged Amzi. Startling Evad and the Knights, though Aweran smiled at her, recognizing her beautiful features.

“Thank you.” She said to Amzi. “Thank you.”

“You’re very welcome, my lady. We’ll need to get you out of here as fast as possible.”

“I understand.”

“I’ll go and get my gear.” Evad said to Amzi. “I’ll meet you guys out in the parking field.”

“Do hurry.”

“I surely will.”

Evad walked through the corridor and found himself surrounded with patrolmen in every corner.

“I’ll be damned.”

A few patrolmen approached him. Evad smiled as he walked toward the elevator, going back up to the top floor. The patrolmen continued to look on toward him as the elevator doors closed.

“I’m a free man gentlemen.” Evad said. “Can’t place me back in your cells.”

“What’s that supposed to mean?” A patrolman said.

“Just some cocky prick.” Another patrolman said.

Amzi, Aweran, and the Knights lead the young woman toward the elevator, passing by the patrolmen. They noticed the young lady with them and stepped in fromt of Amzi.

“Why is she out of her cell?”

“We came here to bail her out.”

“That’s not what the upper office sent to us. You were sent to release an Evad Nod.”

“That is true, but, we’re getting a double release this

day. Evad Nod and this young lady. Check your system to see the information.”

The patrolmen gazed at the monitor, searching the information. After reading it, they turned to Amzi and nodded.

“Our apologizes, sir.”

“It is all well.” Amzi said. “You were just doing your job.”

On the upper floor, Evad walked toward the closet section, where the equipment and gear that belongs to the prisoners is being kept. He searched the closet, which was designed in an alphabetical fashion.

“Where are the Ns?” Evad said. “I am looking for the Ns.”

He walked through the closet, until finding the N section and looked through the drawer, finding his black hat, black trench coat, and range, an energy blasting pistol.. Evad smiled.

“Finally. My baby back into my hands.”

Evad put on his belt and holster, where the range went. He put on his trench coat and hat and exited the closet section. Upon exiting the closet, Evad noticed Dos Ar-Suyaza standing at the counter speaking with the woman at the desk, behind the woman stood four rainshockers.

“This isn’t a good sign.”

“May I ask who you are looking for?” The woman at the counter said.

“I am wondering if any gentlemen came pass here.” Dos said. “They wore robes with cloaks. One in particular speaks in a philosophical manner.”

"Yeah. We did have some men walk in that fit the description."

"Where have they gone?"

"They were down on the third floor."

"Thank you very much."

Evad went to the elevator and before the doors closed, Dos and the rainshockers walked in and stood next to him. The elevator doors shut as Evad stared at Dos and the rain shockers.

"Looks to me like someone is in trouble." Evad said.

Dos looked at him with disgust, to which Evad only smiled at her.

"It is none of your concern, enashian." Dos said. "I am on orders from a high source."

"I can tell. You have his shockers walking alongside you to your command."

"What do you know of rainshockers?"

"I know they can be a pain in the ass for one."

Dos smirked. Taking some little enjoyment out of Evad's sarcasm.

"Tell me, have you seen any Knights roaming around here?"

"Not to my understanding."

"Are you sure you're telling me the truth?"

"Basically I can say that I am."

On the third floor, Amzi and the Knights stood in front of the elevator doors, awaiting for them to open. Aweran stood next to the young lady, interested in speaking with her.

"You can say something." She said.

"Oh. I didn't want to just start talking out of nowhere

is all.”

“What is your name?”

“Aweran Serkelrod. You can just call me Aweran. What is your name?”

“Zeena Lyh, I’m from the planet Endor.”

“The planet where the Carus Sword is kept hidden?”

“Yeah. I’ve seen the ancient home of the legendary Siegfried-Ard.”

“What’s it like?”

“It’s a calming place. The peace there is nice until its trampled upon by outsiders seeking the Carus Sword.”

“Do you know where the sword is located?”

“No. but I’ve heard its buried beneath the Conscendo Sceleratus.”

“The mountain of the Ard Family.”

“Yeah.”

The elevator doors opened and both side were immediately at arms with each other. Amzi looked at Evad in the elevator, standing on the side of Dos.

“What is going on, Evad?”

“Tell me about it.”

Dos stepped out of the elevator and faced the Knights with the rain shockers surrounding them. She smiled as she looked into the eyes of the Knights and stopped on Amzi.

“The legendary Amzi Grake.” Dos said. “It is a pleasure to meet you finally.”

“Who are you, huntress?”

“You may call me Dos Ar-Suyaza. I am here on duty for the Viper Order. Sinth Cain and Sinth Kara require that I eliminate you and your fellow brethren from existence.”

“You will find out that it isn’t an easy task to accomplish.”

“I’m aware of that, Abhdi Knight.”

"KNIGHTS!" Amzi yelled, with the knights raising up their aduroblades.

The Knights slaughtered the rainshockers within seconds with the aduroblade as Aweran and Zeena stood back from the fight. Evad signaled to them to enter the elevator. They ran for it while the Knights fought off the patrolmen. Once the patrolmen were defeated, Aweran and Zeena made it to the elevator. They now awaited Amzi and the Knights to enter. In their way stood Dos, who reached to her side, revealing an adurowhip in her possession. The adurowhip was made of a metallic leather material and glowed a neon blue and was surging with energy. Amzi nodded at her while gazing at the whip.

"You came prepared, huntress."

"As I always do."

Dos swung her adurowhip across the floor around the Knights as they fought off the whip with the aduroblades. They ducked and swiped the Dos' adurowhip several times to avoid an attack.

"Go to the ship!" Amzi said. "We'll be there shortly!"

"Are you sure, master?" Aweran said.

"I am sure. Now go."

The elevator door shut while the Knights battled Dos. She swung her adurowhip toward Ebed's aduroblade, which wrapped around it. Ebed pulled his blade closer, pulling Dos near them. Novad ran toward Dos and smacked her in the head with his forearm. Dos fell to the ground, releasing the grip on the adurowhip, which fell to the ground.

"Let's go." Amzi said.

The Knights went through the elevator, making their way to the ship. Aweran, Zeena, and Evad stood by the ship, awaiting Amzi and the Knights to approach them.

"What's taking them so long?" Evad said. "They

should've been out here by now."

"Give them a few moments." Aweran said. "They'll be here soon."

"I hope so. Wait, who the hell are you, kid?"

"Someone they need for assisting their mission."

"Is that right?"

"It is. Ask them when they get here."

"I will. We'll see which of us they'll need the most."

"That right?"

"Damn right, kid."

"Don't start some competition over who is needed the most while I'm around." Zeena said. "Keep yourselves focused on the real issues."

"Fair enough." Aweran said.

"Yeah." Evad said. "Listen to the lady, kid. You can learn something from a woman."

"As if you would know."

"I know as much as I need to know."

"Ugh, enough." Zeena said. "Quit your bickering."

From the entrance doors came Amzi and the Knights, who ran toward the ship. The ship opened, which Aweran, Zeena, and Evad entered into it with the Knights following.

"Its about time you guys showed up." Evad said. "Can we leave this damn place now?"

"Surely." Amzi said. "Everyone buckle yourselves up. We're going hyper speed in a matter of moments."

While the ship began to hover into the air above the prison, Dos walked outside and seen the ship above her.

"Damn Knights!" She yelled as the ship flew away into hyper speed.

V
THE INWARD BEING

With the Helio Sor flying through the outer depths of space on autopilot, Amzi walked toward the middle of the ship where the Knights sat with Aweran, Zeena, and Evad.

"Aweran and Zeena, come over here." Amzi said. "I have much to discuss with the two of you."

Aweran and Zeena sat in the front of Amzi with the Knights sitting behind him and Evad sitting next to the pilot door, chewing some gum that was left in his belt pocket.

"There is a reason why the two of you were chosen. Evad is a needed ally of course, but you two, I can sense the power of the Avior within you both. You just need to learn of its use."

"What do you mean we have the Avior within us?" Zeena said. "I've never heard much of this Avior."

"Now you have that opportunity, young lady. An opportunity that will change your life into something greater than your mind could possibly comprehend."

"What should we know of the Avior, Master?" Aweran said.

"First things is you both must learn how to communicate with it. The Avior speaks to you in your mind and gives you guidance in all of your ways. With its guidance, you can accomplish great things in your lives and make others better for it."

"That is why I turned it down some years back." Evad said smacking on his gum. "I can't help but scoff at the idea of helping others when they never helped you in a circumstance."

"You're a smuggler, old friend." Amzi said. "That is why you've never come to learn of the power of the Avior."

Evad laughed hysterically. "No disrespect of course, but I'd rather have my trust in my range rather than pocus spiritualism and ancient weapons."

"In time, you will learn how often the Avior has spared your life from those who possess the Dekar."

"When I do, old friend, let me know."

"What is with your attitude?" Aweran said to Evad.

"There's nothing wrong with my attitude, boy." Evad said. "Maybe you should learn from me one thing in particular."

"What is that?"

"Don't give a shit about anybody but yourself and your deeds. That is the only way you'll stay focus on the matters that truly need managing."

Amzi shook his head and glanced at the Knights, who are already tasting distain at the sight of Evad Nod. Evad looked toward them and nodded his head sarcastically.

"You'll have to deal with me until your little mission is complete, boys."

On the other side of outer space, Dos makes her return to Moraltis, where she stands in the throne room facing Sinth Cain and Sinth Kara. Both of whom look at her with questioning.

"Huntress, have you completed the task which was

given into your hands?" Sinth Cain said.

"I found the Knights as you both requested, masters."

"So, where are their remains, huntress?" Sinth Kara said. "What of the whereabouts of the Knights' aduroblades?"

"The Knights were more powerful than I perceived them to be. They showed no fear and took out the rainshockers that came along with me in a quickening. I took it to fight them myself, but they overpowered me and knocked me unconscious."

"The Knights are still free, roaming the universe is what you're telling us, huntress?"

"That I am telling you both, masters."

Sinth Cain stood up slowly from this throne and approached Dos. He walked around her, circling her body, rubbing his hand around her blue hair and slowly touching her bluish pale skin. Sinth Kara turns her head away at the sight of Sinth Cain's doings.

"I am a merciful ruler, huntress." Sinth Cain said. "I will give you another opportunity at completing this task we've given you."

"I will highly appreciate that, masters." Dos said. "But, I will require another army to accompany me."

"Since the rain shockers weren't up to good use for you, take some of the howlshockers. Their stealth and aerial techniques should prove of a highly good use of searching those Abhdi Knights out from their secret place."

Dos bowed her head toward Sinth Cain and Sinth Kara, "Thank you, masters. I will not let you down this time."

"Please don't, huntress." Sinth Kara said. "Because I will not hesitate at striking you down and going after the Knights with my own power. The Dekar flows through me as of my own blood. Its power gives me the thirst for combat and the lust for murder. If you do not return here with their aduroblades as proof of the Knights' deaths, I will end your life quickly and I shall hunt down those Ancient Knights myself and give pleasure to the Dekar."

"I understand."

Dos left the throne room and outside in front of her ship stand an army of howl soldiers, dressed in their black and gray uniforms with their militarized goggled helmets, their eyes covered in shadow. Their weapons are solid black and are covered with cloaking tech. After Dos left the throne room, Sinth Cain turned to his wife. She looked at him and could sense the Dekar flowing through him. Rising up within his being.

"The next time you let your tongue roam free in such a manner in front of me, it will be the last thing you decide to do in my presence."

"Do you not understand that I am your wife, Cain. We both are equals in this matter of the Viper Order. We are both Viper Lords and our armies obey us, not one or the other."

"You do not know your place truthfully."

"Don't speak of truth, Cain. As if you are the prime example of such a thing."

Sinth Cain stood up from his throne seat and left the throne room, leaving Sinth Kara by herself as she mediated on the words she and Cain spoke to each other.

Back on the Helio Sor, the Knights speak with Aweran and Zeena about the use of the Avior and the power that it brings upon those who receive it. Novad tells them of the way in acquiring the Avior.

"Die to ourselves?" Aweran said. "How are we to do that?"

"It is an obstacle that lies within you as it does with all living beings in the universe." Novad said. "Once you die to yourself and mortify the deeds of the body, you will receive the Avior and you will have power beyond what you can comprehend."

"How long would such a thing take?" Zeena said.

"It depends on how long you choose to not die to yourselves. Its all in your doing and in your power."

"Sometimes we call the Avior the inward being." Ebed said. "Because it truly lives within you and will truly guide you in all your steps."

"How would we know that we're received the Avior within us?" Aweran said.

"You will begin to speak in a language not known of any living beings within the universe. It is a language from the High Place."

"The High Place?" Zeena said. "What High Place are you speaking of?"

"Caelum." Amzi said. "He's speaking of the high planet that we call Caelum, which is currently at war with a malevolent entity who desires to claim the universe and all life for himself."

"Have any of you been to Caelum?" Aweran said.

"Some of their friends have been there and are still there." Evad said. "I'm sorry, but it is the truth."

"It is best that you keep your mouth closed until you are spoken to, old friend." Amzi said. "Do not utter another word or I will shut your mouth permanently."

"Fair enough, old friend. I need to eat and drink my fill."

Amzi turned from Evad and back to Aweran and Zeena with a smile on his face.

"Aweran and Zeena, in time when we have fully

trained you in the arts of the Avior and when you both receive it within yourselves, then we will present to you to true weapon of an Abhdi Knight."

Amzi commanded the Knights to make some space in the room of the ship and handed Aweran his aduroblade and Ebed gave Zeena his aduroblade. They both stood in the middle of the room with Evad watching from a distance. Amzi stood by them, fixing their stance as they held the aduroblades in their hands.

"What you both hold in your hands are the true weapons of an Abhdi Knight." Amzi said. "The aduroblades are an ancient invention, created during the beginnings of the Battle of Caelum and are still in use to this day. It is known the aduroblades were first created for the Celestials of Caelum. The aduroblades were carry are physical replicas of their own blades."

Aweran and Zeena slowly move around their wrists to gain some balance and control with the aduroblades. Amzi and the Knights watch on while Evad placed his hat over his face, falling asleep.

"You'll need to keep your balance tightly when holding an aduroblade." Amzi said. "For if you were to make a single mistake, it could cost you your life and you could be on your way to Caelum for all eternity. That is if you possessed the power of the Avior within your being of course."

Colliding the two aduroblades against each other. Giving off the sound of a miniature spark with thunder. The flashing light in between the aduroblades gives off the sensation sound of fire meeting energy. They collide the blades again, learning the ways of aduroblade combat.

"Slowly now." Amzi said. "You're not trying to kill each other."

"Yes, Master." Aweran said. "Why do I feel as if I'm

losing a little bit of my breath, Master?”

"The more the blades come into contact with each other, the more oxygen they absorb from the close areas surrounding them. If you were to be in a fight for a period of time, you could lose your breath from the blades."

"Seriously?" Evad said.

"A side effect that comes from the energy coating the blade."

Evad shook his head, whistling from what Amzi had said.

"It's a damn good thing I prefer ranges over ancient blades."

Aweran and Zeena continue to make slow collisions with the aduroblades, learning the ways. Ebed approached Amzi as the training continued.

"Where are we headed, Master?"

"We're going to Dagobar." Amzi said. "We need some weapons to be made."

"Do you think the Grogok Clan will bother to listen to us?" Ebed said. "To make weapons for us?"

"I know they're in a civil war with a neighboring clan." Amzi said. "It shouldn't be much of a problem if we were to give them little assistance in their war."

"I understand your words, Master. How far until we reach Dagobar?"

"Within several hours."

Ebed sat back in his seat as he, Amzi, and the Knights continued to watch Aweran and Zeena learn the arts of the aduroblade. Evad sat by himself in the corner of the room, asleep in a chair. Snoring away.

On the other side of space, Dos flies along the stars in her ship with her new army of howlshockers. The howlshockers cover the entire grounds of the ship from the top to the bottom. The lieutenant howlshocker approached her in the pilot room.

"My lady."

"What have you of information, lieutenant?" Dos said. "Have you located the Knights' location?"

"Not any sort of information yet, my lady. But we have detected some strange energy coming from a distance afar off."

Dos turned to the lieutenant. Intrigued at his words declaring energy afar.

"What kind of energy have you possibly discovered out here in the dark abyss?"

"According to our radars, the energy appears ancient. Very ancient and we're on its trail as we speak."

"It may be them after all." Dos said. "We'll keep tracking this energy signature. It may lead us to those Ancient Knights."

The lieutenant howlshocker saluted and walked away from the pilot room near the other howlshockers in waiting. Dos continued to sit in the pilot seat, placing the ship onto autopilot. She smirked at the possible thought of being on the trail of the Knights and their ship.

VI
NEGOTIATIONS WITH THE ORCHS

The Helio Sor made it way toward the planet of Dagobar within Sector V. A planet covered in lush grasslands and jungles, surrounded with various species of animals and mostly dominated by the Orchs and the Trolls. The Knights look out of the windows of the ship, seeing the greenness of the planet shining through its atmosphere.

"Why are we heading there, master?" Novad said.

"We will need their assistance in the art of weaponry." Amzi said. "They are the best blacksmiths within this galaxy are they not, Knight Novad."

"You have a point, master."

"What kind of weapons will they be making, master?" Orvad said. "Are they for us against the Viper Order?"

"The weapons are for our two young apprentices."

Aweran and Zeena looked at Amzi with a glisten in their eyes. Unaware of the idea of being presented weapons at an early stage in their training.

"Are you sure we'd be needing those weapons at this stage in our training?" Aweran said hesitantly. "We haven't even hit the higher basics yet."

"That is what the outside field is for, Aweran. You will know how to use the *Avior* and its powers when you are on the field facing the enemies whom you have not known."

"Are we going to be on the field on Dagobar?" Zeena

said. "Along with the Orchs and their civil war?"

"That is a possibility that may surely come to pass, my lady. Don't fear the possibility of it. Embrace it so that you can fully learn what it means to be a Knight of the Covenant."

Flying through the Dagobar atmosphere, coming down to the ground, which is covered with hovels and wooden home along with a castle made of a mixture between brick and wood. As the ship hovers down, the Orchs of the Grogok Clan walk out of their homes, wearing fur tunics and apparel. Their skin is gray, almost pale-like and their fangs appear to sit on the outside of their mouths. Their leader, Grodak'Krak walks outside and gazes up toward the ship. He raises up his steel polished sword, slightly covered with dried blood and mucus.

"Who dares invade our land and enters our planet unaware?!" Grodak yelled.

The ship landed on a cliff in front of the Grogok land. The Knights walked out of the ship, with their hands slightly to their sides near the aduroblades. awe ran and Zeena exited the ship. Evad was still asleep until Amzi walked toward him, shaking him.

"Wake up, old friend. We've landed."

"Oh. Well, where are we?"

"Take a look for yourself. You'll be delighted to know."

Evad stretched over toward the closest window he could get to in his seat. Looking outside he immediately sees the Grogok Castle and jumps out of his seat as if electricity had flowed through his body from a lightning bolt. His hat falling to the ship floor, which he picks up and holds looking back at Amzi with a slight sense of fear and anger.

"Why in the hell are we here?!" Evad said. "Dagobar?! Seriously?!"

"It's an important matter why we're here. Calm

yourself, old friend. They will not harm you unless you've done something to them of course."

"I haven't done anything to these orchs. But, I know of their savage civil war. Out of all the planets that are out there, you choose to come here. Abyssus would've been a better place to visit than this."

"I wouldn't be so sure of that, old friend. Dagobar is much more peaceful than Abyssus."

Amzi walked down the steps of the ship with Evad following him, placing his hat onto his head. He walked outside and gazed at the amount of orchs that stood in front of them on the near ground. Evad reached slowly for his range, but Amzi stopped his hand from getting any further.

"Don't you try something stupid, Evad."

"One shot and this can change at the blink of an eye."

"Do not dare to accomplish that idea."

"I'm just being on guard. That's all, old friend."

Amzi moved his hand and continued walking ahead with Evad behind him, his eyes locked on the orchs and their leader. They reached the ground, immediately being surrounded by the orchs. Male, female, children of all shapes and sizes as Grodak'Krak approached the Knights with his sword in hand.

"I recognize such a garb." Grodak said. "You're from the planet called Helio."

"That we are, King Krak." Amzi said. "We are Abhdi Knights of the Covenant. Masters of the Avior. We have come to your planet on an urgent mission and request your assistance in a simple task."

"What task may be of simple reasoning if you couldn't do it yourselves or with your unseen power?"

"Your clan possesses the best blacksmiths of any planet in the universe. We have come to assist an aid in building new weapons for our two young recruits that we have with us.”

Grodak leaned his head over Amzi, looking past him toward Aweran and Zeena. He pointed toward them to come forward, to stand next to Amzi, which they did and stood next to him. Grodak measured both Aweran and Zeena with his sword, waving it around their bodies, measuring their height and arm length.

“These two are Knights of your Covenant as well?”

“They are becoming Knights, King Krak. They will need the appropriate weapon in their defense if they were to become Knights of the Covenant.”

“You speak of your energy blades.”

“That I do.”

Grodak nodded and allowed Amzi and the Knights to enter his castle. They followed him to the inside where they seen the filth of an orch. The amount of trophies that were kept from their enemies troll and orch alike. Some were trophies of gigantic birds and large beasts that roam the planet. Evad looked at the trophies and smiled.

“Looks like you have quite the collection, King Krak.”

Grodak looked at Evad and turned to Amzi, with concern in his eyes.

“Who is this man that has come along with you?”

“He is Evad Nod. A smuggler of sorts. He will be no harm toward you or your clan. Trust my word on that. Otherwise, if he were to do something, you could take care of him yourself.”

“Old friend, that isn’t necessary.”

“It is of necessity if he wishes to have my aid!”

Evad placed his hands up and kept quiet while Grodak lead them toward the blacksmith area of the castle. Walking down a set of stairs, they approach a door, made of wood, which enters into the blacksmith room. Inside were an variety of swords, war hammers, crossbows, machetes, knives, and other sorts of weapons required of the orch's use.

"There is a problem that we have discovered, Knight."

"What problem would that be?"

"We require the usage of the star matter."

"The star matter?" Aweran said. "What is that, master?"

"The star matter is what the energy weapons are primarily made up of. Such is our aduroblades of course."

"You'll have to find some and bring it back to me. That way, I know I can fully trust you and you will have your weapons in no time."

"I wouldn't know where to look for such a particle."

"But, I know of a place, Knight. A place that I wouldn't even dare to step my feet upon its ground or lick its soil."

"What kind of place is it?" Evad said cautiously. " if I may ask?"

"You will have to enter the planet of Ordow to retrieve such a particle, Knight." Grodak said. "That is the last place that I have knowledge of where a star matter is located. In the possession of the Magus Court and the Warlocks of the West Wind."

"The Magus Court has the matter." Amzi said. "I don't know how we can achieve the matter, but we will give it a go."

"A go you will give to it." Grodak said. "I hope you return in one piece and in safe keepings, Knight."

Grodak nodded and allowed them to leave the castle and return to their ship. Once outside, awe ran began to question Amzi of the planet Ordow, the Magus Court, and the Warlocks of the West Wind. Amzi didn't want to give Aweran the answers immediately, but understood that its best for him to know if they enter combat with the Court or the Warlocks.

"I'm just curious to know of them, master."

"I understand and so I will tell you of them."

Amzi sighed as they entered the ship and sat down in the seats. The ship's engine roared as it hovered from the ground and flew away with great speed into the sky, disappearing as if it wasn't there.

"The Magus Court is a vast court of wizards and sorcerers. They do not like to be disturbed by outside forces nor bothered with foreign affairs. Their powers are ones to be reckoned with. They take prisoners only for questioning to kill them afterwards. They are confident in their magic and will not hesitate at putting others in their places."

"What of the Warlocks of the West Wind? Their title sounds very similar to what you descried of the Magus Court."

"True, the wizards and warlocks are somewhat one and the same. But, the Warlocks of the West Wind are far different from the Magus Court. They are an elite group of warlocks whom possess the ability to alter the galaxies of the universe to their command if they do so wish. Within their group, there are four elite warlocks who make the decisions regarding all of their plans. They also have younger warlocks to accomplish smaller tasks that do not require to full attention of the elite ones. What gets me about them is their ability to possess both the Avior and the Dekar at once."

"They hold both the light and dark in their hands?"

"Indeed. They are powerful. If they wanted, they could've ended their war with the Keepers and could've taken over the galaxies within an hour."

"Well, why haven't they done it if they have the power to do it?"

"They fear someone of a higher place. His power is vast enough to eliminate them all in the blow of one swoop. An attack from Him could wipe out the entire warlock elite for ever.”

“Who’s this higher being? I am intrigued to know.”

“I can tell you are, Aweran. But, time will give you the answers you are seeking. When the answers do come to you, it will be as if you’ve already known them. Thanks to the Avior within you.”

Amzi nodded as Aweran smiled to him.

“Meanwhile, you and Zeena must prepare your hearts for the confrontation with the Magus Court. I do not know what will await us on Ordow. Be it our answers being answered or our lives being cut short. I do not know.”

“I will tell her what you have told me, Master. That way she will not be oblivious to what we may come across in Ordow.”

“Do tell her, Aweran and tell her to have faith and let the Avior guide her through the emotions that may cloud her mind given the information that I have given you.”

“I will do so, Master.”

Aweran returned to his seat in the ship next to Zeena. He tells her of all Amzi has told him regarding the Court, the Warlocks, and the planet of Ordow. Amzi can hear every word that Aweran speaks to Zeena and can feel Zeena staying strong throughout the conversation. From the pilot door walks Evad, who sits next to Amzi.

“So, Ordow, huh.”

“Appears to be that way, Evad. You haven’t tampered with the Magus Court have you?”

“I’ve never bothered them with anything. Except maybe a message saying the next time I see one of them, I’m blowing their brains out.”

Amzi shook his head and lowered it down. Evad chuckled for a moment.

“Its only a threat, old friend.”

"Let's hope they do not have memory of the threat you've given them or else you will be the one who's brains are blown out of your head and it won't be by a range or a blade. But, by their magic which is unseen and unheard."

"You don't have to speak to me like I'm a child, old friend."

"Sometimes I think I do."

"Always the elder you are." Evad said as he left the pilot room, returning to his seat in the corner. Amzi placed the ship on auto pilot and laid back in the chair. He closed his eyes and took in a deep breath.

"High One, let the Avior guide us through this unknown tunnel that we approach. For I know, you will be by our side in any matter."

VII
THE SORCERY PLANET

The Helio Sor makes its landfall into Ordow, the planet shrouded with a mystical presence. The colors of blue, red, and violet surround the atmosphere of the planet. Aweran looked out of the window at the planet, amazed at its colors and features.

"It looks so beautiful." Aweran said.

"Do not fall into the easy trap of the planet's mystical illusions, Aweran." Amzi said. "That is the first step to falling into their traps. Most men do not even make it pass this first sight."

"Are you saying those colors are an distraction to pull people away from the real matters of the planet?" Zeena said.

"Indeed they are. Keep your mind guarded and your eyes focused for what you are about to witness."

The ship began to enter the atmosphere, drowning in the colors of the planet. Upon surpassing the colors, they noticed the cold, dark ground that awaits them below on the planet. In the distance can be seen a tower. The tower is dark and built with molten rock, layered in magic walls. The Knights gazed at the sight of the tower and noticed smaller towers were sitting aside the tall one. The clouds appeared to be made of shadow, colored in blue as the sky shined red as if lava were flowing above the atmosphere.

"Do we enter the dark tower, Master?" Aweran said.

"I do not think we should." Amzi said. "The Court will confront us before we find them."

"What happens if we are in a trap and have no way out from the Magus Court?" Evad said. "What of us to do then?"

"We take the fight to them. Be it a necessary precaution against them. Their magic will have to feel our blades. Your range, for you, of course, old friend."

"Where is the location of the star matter, Master?" Orvad said. "Is is somewhere within the dark tower?"

"The Court keeps their items placed in a vault that sits beneath the ground. It would take us to confront their legion of wizards to enter that vault."

"Then we find our way into the vault, master." Novad said. "That way, we can retrieve the star matter and leave this uneasy planet. Its air is soaked in witchcraft."

"That, I can agree with you."

Once the Helio Sor proceeded to land, they stepped out of the ship, looking over the horizon toward the dark tower and the smaller towers. The wind blew through the air, surrounding them as they could feel the magic's power within the air. The scent of the air was that of cinnamon mixed with electricity. The scent entered into their bodies as they could feel the magic becoming stronger with every step they took. Evad kept his hand close to his range as did the Knights with their aduroblades. Aweran held Zeena's hand as they walked toward the towers.

"Don't worry." Aweran said to Zeena. "I will protect you form on here."

"Maybe, I will protect you, young one."

"Funny." Aweran said with a laugh.

Amzi turned toward them. His hand over his mouth, signaling the two to keep themselves quiet. Which they kept quiet.

"This is not the time for such affections, you two." Amzi said. "Keep your focus on why we're here and you will live to see another day."

Evad smirked at Aweran and Zeena. Amzi looked at him, shaking his head.

"Old friend, they are similar to how you behaved during the youth of your days."

"Those times are long gone, Evad." Amzi said. "I am at the age of old now. I have no desire to recite such behaviors as I've done in times past."

"I can see why you wouldn't repeat those acts. But, face it, they're young and they're alive. Its only nature as to what they're doing."

"I am fully aware of such things, Evad. This is not the time to act out those emotions. They can do so when we leave this planet and out of the enemy's hands."

They walked and found themselves at a gate. The gate was made of magic bars, covered in magic aura. Amzi went to touch the gate, but the power of the magic pushed him back, causing him to fall. Aweran ran toward him, helping him up to his feet. Amzi patted Aweran on the shoulder and smiled.

"I haven't felt such a force like that in centuries." Amzi said. "We may have ourselves a battle here."

"How can we fight magic if we can't see it with our own eyes?"

"Trust the Avior to guide you in that matter. For it will show you the arts of your enemies and how to overcome them with the power of the Avior."

"I will hope so."

"Hope you and Zeena shall do. Because from the power that surrounds this gate, we may come across the entire Magus Court."

Amzi commands Orvad to strike toward the gate with

his aduroblade. Orvad strikes the gate and its magic slowly weakens. Another strike, the magic continues to weaken. Orvad swiped once more and the gate opened, but not at the hand of Orvad. Amzi knew the Magus Court had been watching them and decided to open the gate themselves, giving them entrance into the magic lands of Ordow.

"It appears they have granted us entrance." Amzi said. "Maybe they demand to seek an audience with us."

"Let's find out, fellas." Evad said. "I'm keeping my hand close to my range. Never know what these mages are up to."

Walking toward the dark tower, which is the command center of the Magus Court, Amzi and the Knights kept guard as they walked through the paths surrounding the smaller towers. Within the smaller towers were wizards and sorcerers in training. Along with some of the minor warlocks. They all kept close by one another as they continued walking up the paths.

"How many do you think live here, Master?" Aweran said.

"Hundreds maybe." Amzi said. "Probably hundreds more than we see with our own eyes."

"Just keep our eyes open as you've said, Master." Zeena said. "We will get pass all of this and collect the star matter."

"That we will accomplish, my lady."

Making their steps closer to the dark tower, they find themselves surrounded in a energy wall made of magic. Amzi and the Knights tried their hardest to break through the wall with their aduroblades, but it proved unsuccessful. They hear footsteps approaching them, looking around and see no one in sight. They turned toward the tower and surrounding them were three wizards of the Magus Court. Cloaked in red and violet robes and hoods, they examined Amzi, the Knights, Aweran, Zeena, and Evad. They spotted their weapons and nodded.

"What are you to make of us, wizards?" Amzi said. "Speak your words now."

"We will take you into our judgment lair, Knights of the Avior." One wizard said. "There, the Court will know of your presence upon our planet."

The wizards teleported themselves along with the Knights into the dark tower. Within a mere second, they were placed inside the judgment lair, surrounded by the entire Magus Court. Amzi looked around and reached for his aduroblade, but it was gone. So was the Knights' aduroblades and Evad's range.

"Those bed timers took my range!" Evad said. "I'm not standing for this kind of shit!"

"You're going to have to deal with it for now, old friend." Amzi said. "Our weapons are in front of their table."

Their weapons laid atop a table near the exit door of the lair. From the door arrived the entire Magus Court, all covered in red and violet robes. They sat around Amzi and the Knights, measuring them and deciphering their attire.

"These robed men are from Helio." A wizard said. "Why are they here on our planet and within our walls?"

"We are here on urgent matters, Magus Court." Amzi said. "If you would just allow us to speak our words, you will have your answers to why you gaze upon us this day."

"Enough words, Abhdi." The Master Wizard said. "You shall speak your words when you are spoken to. You have not been spoken to so far have you."

Amzi stayed quiet as the Court discussed the matters upon themselves, looking at their weapons on the table. The Master Wizard picked up Amzi's aduroblade and measured it.

He could sense a power coming from the blade and looked toward him.

"It seems your kind have continued to keep usage of such a weapon. Tell me, what brings you to Ordow and what is your business here and for?"

"We have come here to collect some star matter."

"Why would you need star matter? What are you planning to do with it? What are you aspiring to create with its power?"

"We need the star matter to develop weapons for our young apprentices. They need them in order to advance to their next stage in becoming Knights of the Covenant."

The Master Wizard looked at Aweran and Zeena. Surprised by the appearance of a female being labeled a apprentice into the Abhdi Knights. He shook his head and pointed toward the two young apprentices.

"Young apprentices you say." The Master Wizard said. "What gives me the notion of a female joining the ranks of the Covenant Knights?"

"The Avior is powerful among her as it is with him." Amzi said. "They will need their weapons to complete their training."

"If the Avior is as powerful as you say within them, how come I only sense its power among you and your three Knights. The Avior truly is powerful amongst the four of you. How come it is not so with these two?"

"They have yet to receive the Avior completely."

"Really? The Avior is powerful amongst them, but they have yet to receive its power completely? How so and why?"

"They have not fully died to themselves to receive the Avior in its complete embodiment."

"What if I were to say that myself and my wizard brothers came up with the decision to kill all of you now and leave your apprentices here to look over your dead bodies? Would they receive the Avior then? Would they fully embrace its power and defeat us in our own planet?”

“Do not listen to his words, both of you.” Amzi said. “He is only trying to stir up your emotions to clash at him. If you were to do so, you would open the door for the Dekar to enter into you. That is something I wished not to happen to either of you. Keep your calm and wait patiently for the Avior to come into you.”

“When will it come to us, Master?” Aweran said. “I feel as if we are ready to receive it as of right now.”

“The High One makes the decision as to who receives it or not. He will be the final judge in that matter. If He sees it within your hearts to receive the Avior, that He will truly give. As he did to us in our days of youth.”

“Are you sure he’s telling you both the truth, young apprentices?” The Master Wizard said. “Are you sure he and his Knights are making up false claims to you? To lead you and your lives astray from the real powers of the universe.”

“What are the real powers of the universe?” Zeena said.

“Magic, my young ones.” The Master Wizard said with a smile. “Sorcery is the true power of the universe!”

“Don’t listen to him!” Ebed said. “Keep your minds on the Avior! It will come to you! Trust me!”

“Don’t trust him!” The Master Wizard said. “Trust in magic. Trust in the power of sorcery to guide your every step in your lives.”

“Young ones!” Novad said. “Listen to Amzi, he’s telling you the truth. The Avior will come to you when it is time. Don’t give in to the words of this mage.”

Evad walked up toward the Master Wizard and raised his hand at him. Smiling toward him. Amzi looked at Evad.

“What are you up to, old friend?”

"I have something in mind." Evad said. "Trust me on this one."

"What do you have to say to me, enashian smuggler?" The Master Wizard said. "What could you possibly say that would make me hinder toward your words? Your words would be only a smear on the ground, waiting for my foot to clear you out."

Evad nodded sarcastically.

"I have a question, Wizard leader." Evad said. "If you could please listen to my words of choice."

"Well then, speak!"

"Ok, ok. I was wondering, since I am not a Knight, nor one of its apprentices, I just figured I could have my range back. If you so please to give it to me."

The Master Wizard commanded one of the wizards to hand him Evad's range pistol. The wizard gave it to the Master, who examined it and grinned facing Evad and holding the pistol.

"This is your weapon of choice, enashian smuggler?!"

"It is. It comes in handy very well. I could show you if you would please let me out of this magic ball of yours."

"Nonsense." The Master Wizard said. "If we were to let you out, you would try to retrieve this primitive weapon and make an attempt at our lives. Nonsense of me to give you release when you aren't even worthy of the word."

Evad turned to Amzi, who looked as if he wanted to punch Evad. Evad shrugged his shoulders.

"Well, I tried something at least."

"Yet you did, old friend." Amzi said. "Now, we must come up with something else besides blowing their brains out."

"Hey, it was a good plan to start with."

"It never was a good plan to begin with, Evad."

The Master Wizard laughed as he looked toward his fellow wizards, who mocked and giggled at the Knights in the magic circle. The Master Wizard quiet the room and looked down at them in the force field of magic.

"What shall we make of them, Magus Court?" The Master Wizard said. "Shall we end their lives as of the others of the past or should we give them what they came here for and let them leave on their way out?"

"Kill them." One half of the Court had spoken.

"Let them live." The other half said. "They will die out there anyhow with the star matter in their possession."

The Master Wizard nodded his head at both side. Deciding amongst them for the final decision. He stood up from his seat, looking down at the Knights below him.

"As of this moment forward, we, the Magus Court, have placed you Knights of the Covenant, your apprentices, and your enashian smuggler to death. Your deaths will be at the hands of the Warlocks of the West Wind."

"No." Zeena said. "This can't be happening right now."

"Have faith, my lady." Amzi said. "The Avior will come to you. Give it some time."

Aweran shook his head as he stared at the Master Wizard. His hands balled up into fists. His anger toward the Wizard clearly showing on his face and his aura was becoming stronger.

"No." Aweran said. "I will slay all of you before you make an attempt at placing any of us to death."

"Is that so, young apprentice of the Knights?" The Master Wizard said. "Very well, show us what kind of power you possess within you."

The ground beneath the lair began to quake as from the opened windows of the lair bolted in a gust of wind. The wind was heavy and it consumed both Aweran and Zeena.

Both could feel the wind enter their bodies and embed itself in their hearts and minds. Both began to sit up and stand upright, not making any movement. Their hair blew along with the wind. The wind's power was strong enough to make a crack into the tower's walls and overturned the table where the weapons were placed. Aweran and Zeena both began to speak in an unknown tongue. The speech was difficult for the Master Wizard and his mages to comprehend, but for the Knights it was understanding.

"They're speaking in the Aviorian language, master." Ebed said. "I think they're receiving it."

Amzi looked at both of the apprentices and gazed up to the Master Wizard before placing his eyes back on Aweran and Zeena. He turned to the Knights with a smile on his face.

"They have received the Avior." Amzi said. "They now have the power."

The wind shattered the magic ball and released them from the small space. Aweran and Zeena looked at each other. Smiling with energy and they nodded to Amzi and the Knights. Evad looked on with a slight concern for his life at the moment.

"The hell is going on?" Evad said. "I wasn't built for this kind of stuff."

The Master Wizard stood up from his seat as the other wizards began to leave the room in fear. Afraid of what gave them the Avior. Though, the Master Wizard stood tall, facing them all.

"What power I sense from the two of you." He said. "The power is strong and it is bound to your spirits. What is that?"

"It is the Avior." Aweran said. "Now, we have control over its power. To do with it as we are given to do so."

The aduroblades returned to the Knights and so did

Evad's range. They grabbed their weapons and entered combat with the wizards. Magic fighting against advanced tech. Evad blasted his range toward the Master Wizard, who deflected the energy beams toward the wall.

"You really believe such a weapon would harm a powerful figure such as myself?!" He said. "Enashians are really ignorant in their own devices."

"At least I tried taking you out, old timer."

The Master Wizard fired magic lighting toward Evad, who dodged it by running and ducking beneath the seats of the Court. While the fighting was taking place, a blast of light flashes into the judgment lair, ceasing all the fighting. Everyone took a look to see where the light had come from and standing in the middle of the lair was an old man, with long gray hair, who wore a worn out dark gray robe and a white cloak. He removed his hood and it was revealed to be Gaulhan the Wizard, a legendary figure who is said to live on the outskirts of Ordow, away from the Magus Court and Warlocks.

"What brings you hear, Old Mage?!" The Master Wizard said.

"I have come to cease this conflict and grant these individual a safe passage back to their ship so they may leave."

"We're not leaving without the star matter." Aweran said. "Where is it located?"

Gaulhan reached into his robe and pulled out the star matter. The matter was glowing brightly, a blue and white aura. As if smaller stars were connected to the matter. He handed it to Amzi who placed it inside his robe pocket.

"Now, leave." Gaulhan said. "Make sure to never return here unless you want to see your lives ended abruptly."

"I will not let them leave this place with that matter alive!" The Master Wizard said.

"That you will do." Gaulhan said, raising up his staff and pointing it toward the Master Wizard, blasting him with a magic energy, causing him to fly out of the window toward the ground beneath.

"Is he dead?" Aweran said, looking out to the Master Wizard's fallen body.

"He lives, young man." Gaulhan said. "But, he is unconscious for the moment. Now, for your sakes, leave this place."

They exited the judgment lair and walked back to the outside where they could see the Master Wizard laying on the ground, unconscious from the fall. walking behind them is Gaulhan, who guides them back to their ship.

"Keep yourselves safe and keep that star matter protected." Gaulhan said. "Be it well with you, Knights."

"We will keep this matter in safe keepings." Amzi said. "Trust in us."

"I will trust in your actions, Abhdi Knight. Not the words you speak toward me."

Amzi nodded. Showing respect to Gaulhan.

"Fair enough."

They entered the ship and prepared for takeoff. The Helio Sor hovered and flew away as Gaulhan watched it disappear into the sky. Gaulhan turned back toward the tower and vanished into thin air.

VIII
THE FINAL PHASE

The Knights make their return to Dagobar. The Orchs of the Grogok Clan were awaiting their return as King Krak stood outside of his castle, watching the Helio Sor make its landing into their area. He could sense a interstellar energy coming from the ship as they proceeded to exit.

"Do you think they have the star matter, my lord?" A Orch soldier said.

"Let us see and find out." Krak said.

Amzi and the Knights approached Krak with the orchs surrounding them once again. Krak looked at Aweran and Zeena, he could sense an energy flowing from their bodies.

"What has become of your two young ones, Knight?"

"They have received the Avior since they believed." Amzi said. "They are now ready for the bigger obstacles in this life."

Krak nodded with respect toward the two. He invited them back into the blacksmith area of the Grogok Castle. Within the area, the blacksmith orchs were prepared to manufacture the weapons Amzi had spoken about. Krak turned toward him with his hand extended out in front.

"The star matter, Knight."

"Right you are, King Krak." Amzi said, handing the star matter to Krak. Krak analyzed the star matter and nodded gently before handing it to his blacksmiths.

"Build the weapons of the Knights." Krak said. "Do it with as much haste as you can conjure up."

"We have time to wait until they are completed of course." Amzi said. "We are not in such a hurry."

"You're sure about that, old friend?" Evad said. "Because I don't feel quite comfortable standing around a bunch a brutish orchs and standing inside their domain makes me feel naked."

"You'll get over it, Evad. Make sure of that."

They waited and waited as the blacksmiths developed the weapons and coated them with the star matter. After about two and a half hours, the blacksmiths walked out of the room to Amzi and the Knights standing in the throne room of Krak. The blacksmiths handed the weapons to Amzi and returned to their room.

"Your weapons are completed, Knight." Krak said. "How do they feel to your liking?"

Amzi examined the weapons and smiled before handing them each to Aweran and Zeena. They grabbed the weapons and stated at Amzi with a slight lost of words.

"These are for us, Master?" Aweran said, glancing at the weapon in his hands. "Seriously?"

"You have received the Avior within you. With that, you are now able to possess an aduroblade of your own. Hence forth, the two of you are now a part of *Those of the Avior*."

Aweran raised up his aduroblade, which was coated in a dark blue energy as the sword appeared to be made of orch metal and energy. Zeena's aduroblade was in fact an adurostaff, which both ends of the staff were coated in a bright green and was made of almost all energy with minor details of steel. They celebrated their elevated status of becoming true Abhdi Knights and Knights of the Ancient Covenant. Krak applauded them, walking down the steps of his throne.

"I see you are happy with your weapons." Krak said.

"Truly, your clan is the best at the art of blacksmith, King Krak." Amzi said. "I thank you for your service in helping us."

"Better of you to choose our aid rather than the aid of the dwarves in Sudravor. Sometimes they can be costly."

"As I have once known."

Amzi and the Knights were ready to leave as Krak escorted them back to the outside. While making their steps toward the outside of the castle, shouts and screams could be heard coming from around the Grogok landscape. They all ran quickly to see what was taking place and right in front of them, in their land was the rival orch clan called the Tukoeater Clan, lead by their leader Sodang Brok. Brok walked with a strut as the skull necklaces and bracelets upon his body rocked along with each footstep he took. Krak roared toward him, holding up his war sword and prepared for combat. Sodang chuckled as behind him approached Dos and her army of howl soldiers.

"Dos has found us." Orvad said. "She has come to our location unaware, master."

"It seems she has forsaken the rain shockers and has been give usage of the howlshockers." Novad said.

Sodang turned to Dos, who stood beside him. Both shook hands as they gazed the landscape of the Grogok Clan.

"It appears you are outwitted, Krak!" Sodang said. "Perhaps, you could prove yourself wise to best me in battle."

"I will tear your head from your shoulders and make the ground drink your blood!"

"So be it."

Sodang roared with his warhammer held high above his head, leading his clan into war with the Grogok Clan.

Behind them run the howlshockers, being commanded by Dos, who ran beside them, yelling as she swung around her adurowhip. Krak and his army of orchs were prepared for the fight. Amzi approached Krak, holding his aduroblade in his hand.

"We will fight with you, King Krak." Amzi said. "It is the best that we can do for you after what you've done for us."

Krak nodded.

"Together we fight, Knights. Together we will win."

The Grogok army was set as was Amzi and the Knights. Aweran and Zeena were also prepared for the fight coming their way. They stood still, concentrating the Avior into the battlefield. The sounds of roars and shouts were coming closer and growing louder by every second that passed them by. The rival clan and the howl soldiers were coming much closer, the intensity that filled the battlefield was as powerful as the ray's of the sun burning through the ground.

"NOW!" Sodang roared.

"SLAUGHTER THEM ALL!" Krak yelled.

The Grogok and Tukoeater clans collided with each other with the force of a mountain ramming into another mountain. Instead both mountains would have cracks growing within them. The armies of both sides smashed each other with their swords and hammers. Others decided to use their fists and teeth to bleed out the opposing clan. Dos and the howlshockers faced down the Knights and Evad. She smiled toward them and noticed the energy soaring from Aweran and Zeena.

"What have they become?" Dos said. "The energy I sense from them is strange and unusually powerful."

"They are Knights of the Covenant." Amzi said. "Like myself and my brothers in arms."

"That makes it much more better to see two more of

you that will meet your ends at the slash of my adurowhip."

Dos commands the howlshockers to attack the Knights and their battle begins with the aduroblades colliding with the energy shields and batons of the howlshockers. Aweran and Zeena surround Dos, who smiles at them both, slashing her adurowhip into the ground, causing a tiny tremor, knocking the both of them off their feet.

"Your newfound power will not save your lives from me." Dos said.

"We will overcome you with our newfound power and you will be the one to fall on this day." Aweran said.

"What he said is true and will come to pass." Zeena said. "Are you ready to meet your end, huntress?"

"Better to worry of your own end rather then the end of mine."

Aweran and Zeena swung their aduroblades to Dos, who grabbed them with the adurowhip and kicked Aweran to the ground. Swinging blows with Zeena until she knees Zeena in the abdomen and tosses her into one of the nearby hovels. Dos smirked, wiping her face from the flying dirt in the air from the battles of the orch clans. Zeena looked up toward Dos, who taunted her arrogantly.

"Stand up, Dame of the Covenant!" Dos said. "Face me like a woman!"

Zeena yelled as she rammed into Dos with her adurostaff and they battled with twists and turns. Aweran went for a slash to Dos, which she jumped over and kicked Aweran in the jaw with the front of her boot. Dos laughed as she blocked the attacks from Zeena's adurostaff.

"They call you Knights?! A fable worth telling the Viper Order."

"You make a joke of us, huntress." Zeena said. "Wait till the universe hears the tale of your defeat at the hands of two novice Knights."

Trees began to crash and fall to the ground while the civil war of the orch clans continued to take place. Krak and Sodang clashing their swords and hammers together with anger flowing through their eyes. Krak kicked Sodang in his knee and jammed his own knee into Sodang's jaw.

"Appears you are weakening, Sodang!" Krak said.

"I am not dead yet, Grodak!" Sodang said. "Now, face me like you mean it or you will see the downfall of your feeble clan!"

Krak roared, slamming his sword against Sodang's hammer continually. The Knights had near defeated most of the howl soldiers, except for three who were highly trained in the art of aduroblade combat. An orch from the Tukoeater clan ran toward the Knights. Ebed swiped the orch in its stomach with his aduroblade, cutting the beast in half. Evad had climbed the castle and took shots down at the battling orchs. Firing his range and blasting orchs in their shoulders, heads, and legs. Evad savored the moment of taking the shots. Laughing as he pulled the trigger.

"I love this kind of shit!"

Evad fired more range blasts until he spotted an orch standing afar off with a cannon. Which he fired and the cannon blasted the wall of the castle where Evad was standing. He ran down the corridor from the falling ground. Evad jumped and grabbed onto the opposite wall as the wall he was once leaning against was falling to the ground in rubble.

"Sure hope no one was standing there."

The land was covered in orch corpses across every corner near the Grogok Castle. Krak and Sodang continued their bout as both leaders were become tired and their stamina was declining. The Knights had finished off the remainder of the howlshockers, which caught Dos' attention as she turned back to face Aweran and Zeena. They stared at her and jolted their hands toward her, giving off an Avior blast, which slammed Dos into one of the hovels, bursting her through its wooden walls. Aweran and Zeena looked at one another as Dos slowly walked out of the crashed hovel, holding her right arm.

"What in the hell was that?!" Dos said. "What kind of power have the both of you consumed?!"

"That was the power of the Avior you have felt, huntress." Aweran said. "Would you like another touch of its power?"

"This war is not yet over." Dos said running back to her ship. Zeena went to chase her, but Aweran held her back.

"She's getting away, Aweran!"

"You'll have another time to stop her." Aweran said. "Trust me. You'll be seeing her again in no time."

The orch armies were all but finished. Not a single orch soldier was standing except for their leader who began to fight near the castle walls. Aweran and Zeena went to aid Krak, but Amzi stopped them.

"King Krak can deal with his rival himself." Amzi said. "His strength has not yet been revealed to us."

Krak swiped his sword at Sodang's hammer, which clashed once more together. Sodang went for a punch and Krak caught his arm, cutting it off with his sword. Sodang roared in pain as he dropped his hammer and fell to his knees. Krak took his sword and impaled Sodang in his chest. Sodang's breath was begging to cease as Krak walked behind Sodang and held his head in between his hands.

"This war between us is over, Sodang!" Krak said, tearing the head of Sodang off from his shoulders. Roaring in victory, holding Sodang's head above him as the blood dripped onto his chest.

The sound of ship had sounded and gathered everyone's attention. The ship was of Dos who was flying away from the land and exiting the planet. Zeena watched as Dos' ship disappeared into the sky.

"Another time, huntress." Zeena said.

Krak approached the Knights with the severed head of Sodang. The Knights nodded to him as they looked around at the decimation of the land. Hovels destroyed, hundreds dead from both sides and the castle wall destroyed.

"Appears that the remainder of my clan have much work to do."

"It is so." Amzi said. "We can help you."

"You've helped me enough, Knight." Krak said. "I thank you for the assistance in ending this civil war."

"The pleasure is ours, King Krak."

From the castle walked out Evad, who stared at the Knights and gestured toward Amzi the wall falling and himself latching onto the edge. Evad approached Krak and patted him on the shoulder.

"Sorry about your wall, your highness." Evad said. "Though, I did what I could to stop the orch who fired the cannon."

"So you say, enash."

Evad walks up to Amzi, looking around at the destruction of the land.

"So, can we go now?"

"Yeah. We can go."

The Knights approached their ship and entered it. Upon preparing for takeoff, the ship's message holder began to beep constantly. Amzi looked at it, uncertain of what is going on with the machine. He pressed the button and arose a red hologram. The hologram was an image of both Sinth Cain and Sinth Kara. Standing on the grounds of a planet.

"Knights of the Ancient Covenant of Elyon." Sinth Cain said. "I have grown tired of chasing you down throughout the sectors of the universe. I have decided through my own power and will, to send you this message of combat. Let us end this thousand age war between us once and for all. Meet myself, my wife, and my army on the planet of Thran. Come and face us, Knights. Protect your unworthy covenant or come to meet your end and watch as the Viper Order grows and consumes all of the universe."

"We await you all." Sinth Kara said. "I hope you can come and greet us. Please, we insist."

The hologram had shut down and the Knights looked at one another. Evad took off his hat and wiped his forehead and exhaled.

"Thran, huh?" Evad said. "That planet of destruction?"

"What do you say of the challenge, Master?" Ebed said. "They want us to go to Thran to meet our deaths."

"Thran is inhabited with destruction and war." Novad said. "It is the primary place to resolve this conflict between us and them."

"We can finally be rid of this Viper Order once and for all, master." Orvad said. "Finish what our ancestors could not."

Amzi looked at Aweran and Zeena. He walked toward them and hugged them both. Not knowing how to response to such an action. They hugged him back.

"What do the two of you suggest we do?" Amzi said. "Shall we proceed to Thran and end the Viper Order for good or shall we decline their offer and have them to continue to chase us down across the universe?"

Aweran and Zeena glanced at each other before facing Amzi. They nodded to him and toward the other Knights.

"I suggest we go to Thran." Aweran said. "End this war

once and for all."

"I agree with Aweran all the way." Zeena said. "Let's go to Thran, Master."

Amzi nodded as he walked back to the pilot seat. The ship takes off and travels into space. Amzi turned back to the Knights sitting amongst each other and smiled.

"To Thran we go." Amzi said. "Aviorspeed."

Across the sectors, the Viper Order had already made their way toward Thran and have landed on the war-torn planet during the warfare on Dagobar. The clouds of Thran are dark and gray as thunder clapped its way across the sky. The ground red and glowing as magma. Walking out of the Viper ship called the Sinth-Tred is both Sinth Cain and Sinth Kara. They turn around to see the massive ship called the Attonbitus arrive and within it are thousands of rainshockers and Imperial Viper Knights, who are dressed in black and red robes with their red aduroblades out. Waiting for the Knights' decision to make itself known.

"Do you think they'll come, my love?" Sinth Kara said.

"For their sake, I hope they never make it here. If they happen to arrive, we know what to do with them."

IX
BATTLE OF THRAN

Sinth Cain and Sinth Kara stand on the grounds of Thran, facing the sky, awaiting the arrival of the Knights of the Covenant. The rainshockers surround the perimeter of the selected battlefield with the Imperial Viper Knights keeping a close distance around the Viper Lords. The area was quiet, except for the occasional thunder claps that would come from the dark clouds above.

"Maybe they won't show themselves at all." Sinth Kara said. "I believe they fear us and they fear the power of the Dekar. What it can do to them as opposed to their Avior power."

"I have told you not to speak so low concerning the Avior, Kara. You do not know its true power."

"I don't think you fully understand what you even possess, my Cain. We possess the power of the Dekar. We are stronger than Those of the Avior and their High One. We are the true dominators of the universe. We are true power."

The clouds clapped with a louder thunder, getting the attention of both Cain and Kara as the Helio Sor makes it way through the clouds, covered in lightning and landing on the red grounds of Thran. The rainshockers raised up their plasma ranges toward the ship and the Viper Knights stood their grounds, holding their aduroblades steady.

"They are arrived." Cain said. "Prepare yourself, Kara.

It is a war that we are about to engage in.”

Within the Helio Sor, Amzi talks with the Knights and Evad about what is to come upon the battlefield of Thran. They join hands and gather together in a prayer. Silencing themselves within. Amzi speaks to the High One, to let the Avior flow through them all in order to gain the victory against the Viper Order. They release their hands as the ship’s door opened. They walked out, seeing the Viper Lords and their army standing before them.

“The Knights have answered our calling.” Cain said.

“We are here as you asked, Sinth Cain.” Amzi said. “What have you to say now?”

“What do I have to say? I say, we end this conflict between our forces. Finally bringing peace into the universe for the generations coming behind us.”

Amzi measured Cain’s words. Noticing a strange conflict taking place within Cain’s own being.

“You talk as if you’re a different breed of Viper Lord. What has become of you? Something has transpired in your spirit.”

Kara turned to Cain and glared toward Amzi. Her eyes fired up with rage toward the Knights. Her pupils began to glow red as she raised up her own aduroblade and yells at them with a loud scream.

“We destroy these feeble Knights once and for all!” Kara said. “We make sure the Dekar rules the universe for ever!”

Throughout the sky appeared a variety of Eglahs, the round and pointed starfighter ships of the Viper Order. Kara gazed up toward them and smiled, showing the Knights her smile. Amzi nodded and point up above them. Kara looked around them as did Cain.

"We did not come alone."

From above the Knights came down the Emerald Cavalier Force, wearing their green and black uniforms and shaded in their glowing green aura along with the Revolter Squadron, flying down with their Aver-Wings, Xathos-Wings, and Yavos-Wings. Being lead by their captain in the Ark-Celeritas, the leading starfighter of them all.

"You have your fighters of the air." Amzi said. "As do we."

"Enough of this nonsense!" Kara said. "My love, let's take the battle to them. Kill them all and end this period!"

"As we shall, my queen." Cain said.

Cain turned toward the rainshockers and the Viper Knights. He raised up both the Sinthblade and his aduroblade in the air and pointed them toward the Knights.

"Wipe them out." Cain said. "All of them."

The rainshockers ran toward the Knights as did the Viper Knights, who lead the way into battle. Cain and Kara walked behind the rainshockers, their weapons prepared for battle. Amzi turned to Aweran and Zeena. Each of the Knights have their aduroblades out and ready. Evad stood steady with his range in hand.

"This is gonna get ugly." Evad said. "But, I like ugly."

"Are you both ready for this?" Amzi said.

"We are, Master." Aweran said. "We both are ready."

Amzi nodded and raised up his aduroblade.

"For the High One!" Amzi said.

The Knights ran toward the Viper Knights with the rainshockers behind. The Eglahs flew in the air toward the Emerald Cavaliers and Revolter Squadron. The battle began on the ground with the Knights clashing aduroblades with the

Viper Knights. Evad fires toward the rainshockers, hitting them in their heads and chests. Amzi and the three Knights battled the Viper Knights on their own. Aweran and Zeena both stood, swiping at the incoming rain shockers, looking pas them toward Cain and Kara.

"It seems the two want us." Kara said. "Shall we give us over?"

"We shall." Cain said.

Aweran and Cain ran toward each other as did Zeena and Kara. Both sides engaged in aduroblade combat with Aweran having to use the Avior to guide him in facing Cain with both the Sinthblade and aduroblade. Kara swung her aduroblade, colliding with Zeena's adurostaff. Zeena kicks Kara in her leg and punches her.

"What strong feats you have, little Zeena."

"I've waited for this moment a long time." Zeena said. "You kept me locked away in that prison on false charges."

"It was the only way to get you away from the truth and grow further to the lie."

"Your attempt didn't work. I've come much closer to the truth thanks to you."

"How dare you."

Both clashed their aduroblade and adurostaff. The energy coming off the blades was strong enough that it started to burn the air around them. Aweran continued to swing around his aduroblade against Cain's Sinthblade and aduroblade. Cain laughed as the two were in combat.

"I feel the Avior within you, boy!"

"It gives me the strength to end your reign of destruction."

"My reign will live on through the power of the Dekar!"

The ships of both sides continued to battle in the air.

Blasting energy beams into the opposing ships, crashing them down to the Thran grounds. From the air, comes down another ship, the ship of Dos. She witnesses the sky battle as well as the ground battle. She lands her ship and jumps out of it, running toward Zeena and Kara with her adurowhip in hand. Twirling the adurostaff toward Kara, Zeena turns and is speared by Dos, who holds her to the ground. Going for a series of punches which Zeena dodges every one of them and blasts Dos off of her with the Avior power. Kara goes for a stab, but is stopped by Zeena's adurostaff.

"It won't be that easy."

Aweran and Cain continued their fierce battle. Swiping the aduroblades against each other, giving off sparks of energy. Falling to the ground and burning it within seconds. Aweran kicked Cain and swiped the Sinthblade from Cain's right hand.

"One blade down." Aweran said. "One more to go."

"You think I can't take you with just the aduroblade. You are surely mistaken. I am a Viper Lord for a reason."

Both clashing their aduroblades against each other. Having out a test of strengths, trying to shove the other back and onto the ground. Cain laughs throughout the entire bout. The dog fights in the air between the Squadron and the Eglahs continue with their captain giving commands to attack the Attonbitus, which is the command center for the Eglahs. Vulture Drone come flying out of the Attonbitus and toward the starfighters, crashing into them without notice.

"Change of plans!" The Captain said. "Fire your energy toward the Vulture Drones. They are suicidal drones!"

Members of the Emerald Cavalier Force fly toward the Vulture Drones, grabbing them by their heads and ripping them apart before taking out other Eglahs around them. One Eglah swoops past an Emerald Cavalier, puling off the medallion from his neck, suddenly falling to the ground before being caught by another Emerald Cavalier.

"Not yet."

The Cavalier retrieved the other's medallion. Handing it back to him as he placed it own, gaining back his Emerald powers. Flying towards the Eglah which swooped by. On the ground, the rainshockers were dying from the crashing ships and firing shots from Evad. Some died from making an attempt toward the Knights who have nearly defeated the Viper Knights except for a few.

"There's only three more of them, master." Ebed said.

"We take them out." Amzi said. "Get rid of them completely."

The Knights battled the Imperial Viper Knights, clashing aduroblades and fighting with their legs and arms to finish them off. Zeena swung her adurostaff against both Kara and Dos who decided to team up against her. Zeena twirted the adurostaff, knicking Kara to the ground with the Avior blast and impaling Dos with the adurostaff. Dos fell to her knees, dropping her adurowhip.

"I told you." Zeena said.

Dos fell to the grounds of Thran and died. Zeena and Kara continued to battle each other. Both becoming tired. Aweran and Cain were slowly becoming worn out, clashing their aduroblades constantly and trying to gain oxygen in their surroundings as the blades were consuming the air around them.

"I can feel you wearing out, boy." Cain said. "I have the advantage of this battle now!"

"I think not." Aweran said. "I still have the power of the Avior to aid me."

Cain swung his aduroblade, knocking the blade out of Aweran's hand and raised up his left hand, attacking him with the Dekar Lightning. The red lightning, glowing darkly and quickly consuming Aweran as he screams out in pain. Falling to his knees.

"They didn't teach you the difference of feats between the Avior and the Dekar did they, boy?!"

Aweran tries to fight back, but is unable to retrieve his aduroblade laying on the ground. Cain laughed as he continued blasting him with the Dekar Lightning. Aweran laud still on the ground as Cain raised up his aduroblade above Aweran.

"Now, you will understand the true power of Those of the Dekar!"

Cain went for a slash, but Aweran moved out of the way as the ground began to quake. Everyone on the ground had ceased fighting. Feeling the strength of the quake becoming stronger and they happen to notice they were fighting near a volcano. The volcano began to shake. The volcano had a release of magma come down and the center had burst open. The magma from the volcano flowed throughout the battlefield and entered into the sea of Thran that laid nearby the ships. With the magma entering the sea, the waters began to boil and from the waters sounded off a roar. Everyone turned to the waters and from them arose the Thran Beast. A large dragon that lived beneath the sea.

The Thran Beast, thought to be only of myth had risen out of the sea. Its scales colored in black and red and its eyes appeared as if they were fire surging within them. Its loud roar ceased the thunder in the clouds as it flew out of the sea and toward the battlefield. Exhaling streams of fire from its mouth toward the ground. Burning the remaining rainshockers. Remnants of the fire had slightly touched both Aweran and Cain, burning their uniforms and flesh.

The Thran Beast flew into the air and entered the dog

fights between the ships with its wings knocking both the Eglahs and Vulture Drones to the ground. The Ark-Celeritas flew past the Thran Beast, almost colliding into its side. The captain shook his head.

"What the hell was that thing?!"

Amzi and the Knights watched the Thran Beast fly through the air, destroying ships in its path.

"I thought the creature had died out centuries ago." Novad said.

"Appears that it lives and it is angry." Amzi said. "Let us finish what we've come for."

Kara was stuck between some debris from the crashed Eglahs. Zeena approached her and went to kill her, but stopped herself. Kara became angry as Zeena's ceasing. Shaking the debris around her.

"You better kill me!" Kara said with a sinister laugh. "You better kill me, Zeena!"

"No. I won't do it. I won't become what you've already made yourself into."

"You petite fool!"

Zeena walked away as Kara continued to yell at each. Screaming for her to kill her. Aweran and Cain continued the battle, even after being weakened by the fire of The Thran Beast. Cain quickly went for a swing, but Aweran raised up his palm, stopping Cain's swing with the Avior and retrieved his aduroblade from the ground to the side. Aweran held his aduroblade and swiped it against Cain's chest. Cain stood frozen as he stared at Aweran. He turned, facing Kara, who could sense his life flowing out of him.

"NO!" Kara yelled.

Cain fell to the ground, presumably died as his chest slowly was opened in half. Kara screamed as she blasted the Eglah debris from around her and ran toward Aweran with her aduroblade.

"You will pay for this!" Kara said.

She ran toward Aweran and tripped her foot on a rock and fell into a sharp metal that was once a Vulture Drone. Kara's head fell against the drone debris, to which she had knocked herself out instantly from the impact. Aweran gave off a sign of relief and as he went to turn to Zeena, a shadow figure manifested before him. Only he could see the figure, which was shrouded in shadow. A fog of smoke, difficult to see through.

"Who are you?" Aweran said.

"You. You!." The shadow said. "The Avior has made you powerful. But, I sense something else within you. The Dekar."

"The Dekar doesn't have a place within me. Only the Avior does."

"Not as of this moment. The Avior yet lives within you, but your aggression, your focus is giving in to the Dekar. In time, you will learn to receive it and use it along with the Avior. Both powers of light and dark, within your grasp. Seize it, Aweran and you will become more powerful than anyone you've known. Even the Knights and even Amzi Grake. Imagine the power you could possess within your hands. Within your mind. Within your spirit.."

"I won't listen to this."

'You won't as of this moment. But in time, you will know that I am right."

"Who are you?!"

"I am a friend. A close friend. We will meet soon. Very soon."

The shadow evaporated as Amzi and the Knights approached him. Seeing Aweran startled a bit. Amzi placed his hand on Aweran's shoulder and smiled.

"The battle is over." Amzi said. "We have one."

"Seems we have, Master." Aweran said with a faint smile.

Evad walked up to Aweran and shook his hand.

"Didn't know you could handle yourself so well."

"The Avior lead me through."

"Nah! You did it!"

"No, Evad. The Avior lead me through the battle. Without it, I would've died."

"If you say so, kid."

The Ark-Celeritas landed as the captain approached Amzi and the two shook hands.

"We've won, Captain."

"We have." The Captain said. "Anytime you need our assistance, we will be there."

"I will count on it."

The Revolter Squadron and Emerald Cavaliers left the planet as did the Knights. Later, a ship landed on Thran, with a hooded figure walking through the battlefield, seeing the dead bodies of those that fell and approaches the body of the presumed dead Sinth Cain and the unconscious Sinth Kara. The hooded figure reaches down and picked up both the Sinthblade and their aduroblades. His crew of imperial rain shockers picked up Cain and Kara, returning them to his ship which flies out of Thran with the Thran Beast looking out at the horizon within the seas. Snarling as it sucked its head beneath the dark waters.

A short period of time after the battle of Thran, the Knights made their return to Helio in the city of Tropolton. The city restored with its people and Aweran and Zeena being made official Knights of the Covenant. With the inclusion of Aweran and Zeena, Amzi names them all Knights of the Advanced Covenant. Outside of the temple, Aweran and Zeena stood together, holding hands and kissing as the Helio sun set before them.

Amzi walks out of the temple and notices the two and smiles. Ebed walks up behind him, looking at the two young Knights standing together. Happiness flowing from within their being.

"So, this is the restoration of all things that was spoken of?" Ebed said.

"No, Ebed." Amzi said. "This is a new beginning of things to come.

ABOUT THE AUTHOR

Ty'Ron W. C. Robinson II is the author of several works of fiction. Including the *Dark Titan Universe Saga* series (*Dark Titan Knights, The Resistance Protocol, Tales of the Scattered, Tales of the Numinous, Day of Octagon*) and *The Haunted City Saga* series. Also of other books (*Lost in Shadows, Hod, The Book of The Elect, Symbolum Venatores, etc.*) and One-Shot short stories More information pertaining to the author and stories can be found at darktitanentertainment.com.